Fiction
Kaye, Gillian.
Waiting for Matt

WAITING FOR MATT

Nicola first met and fell in love with Matthew Hunter when she was eighteen and with him at art school. But then their lives took different directions; Nicky became a successful painter, and Matt the owner of two art galleries. It was fifteen years later that Nicky met Matt again at the opening of his new London gallery. Would sparks still fly or could they manage to be 'just good friends'?

GILLIAN KAYE

WAITING FOR MATT

Complete and Unabridged

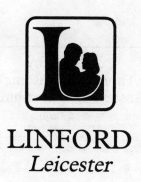

LINFORD
Leicester

First published in Great Britain in 1994 by
Robert Hale Limited
London

First Linford Edition
published 1996
by arrangement with
Robert Hale Limited
London

The right of Gillian Kaye to be identified as
the author of this work has been asserted by
her in accordance with the
Copyright, Designs and Patents Act, 1988

British Library CIP Data

Kaye, Gillian,
    Waiting for Matt.—Large print ed.—
Linford romance library
    1. English fiction—20th century
    I. Title
823.9′14 [F]

ISBN 0–7089–7925–4

Published by
F. A. Thorpe (Publishing) Ltd.
Anstey, Leicestershire

Set by Words & Graphics Ltd.
Anstey, Leicestershire
Printed and bound in Great Britain by
T. J. Press (Padstow) Ltd., Padstow, Cornwall

This book is printed on acid-free paper

1

NICOLA knew very few people in the crowded gallery but she wandered slowly about, glass of wine in hand, pausing when a particular picture caught her eye. The occasion was the opening of the Orion Gallery in London and Nicola was new to the London art world. She had, in fact, arrived in the capital and set up her studio only three weeks previously; this was her first venture into the world she was going to come to know so well.

Suddenly across the crowded, noisy room, through the high-pitched, over-enthusiastic voices of socialite art lovers, through the flash of the press cameras, and through a maze of unknown faces, Nicola saw a face she knew well. Or had known, for it was now nearly fifteen years since she had seen that face but how could she forget the handsome smile, the animated expression, the black hair now tinged with grey of Matthew Hunter?

It is Matt, she said to herself, almost speaking out loud in her surprise. An older Matt but he could not be mistaken and she wondered why she should be so surprised. It would be natural to find Matt at the centre of the London art scene.

He was talking and laughing with an older man whom Nicola recognised as one of the art critics on a national daily paper; she watched fascinated, Matt did not look in her direction and she could watch unseen and unnoticed. And as she watched, the same bewitching personality who was Matthew Hunter transported her backwards in time, back to a time when they had been students together, back to a time when she had been desperately in love with him, back out of that noisy room to the cold, northeast of England, to Newcastle where Nicola had been doing her foundation course at the school of art.

She had arrived in Newcastle at the age of eighteen straight from school in Hexham. And Nicola had been a beautiful young girl at eighteen, her fair hair straight almost to her waist, her blue eyes alive with the enthusiasm and vivacity of youth, her mouth set strong and decided but easily curving into a smile, her whole personality bubbling with the creativeness of her artistic nature. She was a painter, she wanted to be a painter and she had come to college to learn the techniques of being a painter.

Immediately she had been plunged into a world which her sedate girls' school had never prepared her for. The young men were strong-willed, talented and wild; the girls were pretty, flirtatious and clever, but they all shared a friendship and liking towards the shy Nicola. They all worked hard and they celebrated their few spare moments with the little money they had to spare from their grants by meeting and having a drink at the local pub and with hilarious parties at various student rooms in the houses they shared.

Nicola met Matt on the second day; he must have been there on the first but she had been confused and bewildered by all the introductory lectures and had hardly noticed her fellow students.

When she arrived at college the following morning, it was to find a group of them in vociferous argument in the glass-panelled entrance hall of the large building. She stood on the edge of the group to try and find out what it was all about, her eyes being drawn as by a magnet to the male student who was speaking above the others and who seemed to be the instigator of the meeting.

He was very tall to start off with, and his height and the raven black of his hair and his flashing, dark eyes would have set him apart in any gathering. Nicola listened to what he was saying.

"Well, I think one of us should go

and tell Mr Strickland what we think, it's no use just grumbling and doing nothing about it." He looked from one of them to another and suddenly seemed to catch Nicola's eye, for she too, was tall and with her bright, fair head, easily stood out in a crowd.

The young man pointed to her. "You there, with the long, fair hair, what's your name? Tell us what you think?"

Nicola swallowed hard, why ever had he singled her out? But she tried to conquer her shyness and spoke out feeling quite proud of herself for speaking so clearly.

"I'm Nicola Greenhowe, I've only just come so I've no idea what the meeting is about."

"Hallo, Nicola, I'm Matt," was the reply from the devastatingly attractive student. "Some of us think there are too many in the drawing class and that it ought to be split into two. Do you agree?"

She could answer honestly. "Well, yes I do agree, I thought it was too

5

many yesterday, but I don't see how they can split the class if there's only one teacher."

There was a general hum of agreement then another girl spoke up.

"I think we're all in agreement that it's too many but it may be that we've come from schools where there were just one or two of us in a class and now we've got to get used to bigger classes at college."

"Thanks, Elaine, I think you've got a point there. But has anyone got any ideas for dealing with the problem?" Matt was looking round seriously at them and when Nicola found herself raising a hand, he smiled at her.

"Well, Nicola, you don't seem to be afraid of speaking up."

Nicola was marvelling at herself, a confidence which seemed to emanate from Matt himself seemed to have suffused her. "Couldn't we divide the class into two sections and have Mr Strickland instruct us on alternate days, leaving one half to work on their own for some of the time? We could get a lot of work done and wouldn't lose out on the teaching."

A murmur went round the group and Matt was again smiling at Nicola. "Good girl, come up here, and Elaine."

Nicola reluctantly went forward and found herself standing with Matt and Elaine in front of the others. He said something to each of them quietly and then spoke out in his clear, authoritative voice.

"You all seem to agree with what Nicola has suggested, hands up if you think it's OK for the three of us to go and see Mr Strickland."

It was all agreed, the matter was settled with the lecturer and Nicola found that she had a friend in Matthew Hunter. He sought her out at lunch-times and at the end of the week asked her to go out for a drink with him.

In the small, smoky, crowded town pub, Nicola sat bewitched. She was dressed in a deep blue sweater over her jeans and the colours accentuated the blue of her eyes and Matthew seemed equally fascinated. They found they had a lot in common as both came from small country towns in the north and each of them had a parent who was a teacher; Matthew's home was in Ripon. And they found plenty to talk about as each had different aspirations, Nicola wanted to set up her own studio while Matt wanted to go on and read art history at university with the ultimate ambition of becoming a director of an art gallery. He knew he had talent as a painter but could see no future in it and he was ambitious.

Halfway though that first evening and the one drink each that they could afford, they discovered that they had rooms in houses in adjacent streets not far from the college so it seemed natural for Matt to walk home with Nicola and for them to have coffee in her room.

They were a natural and striking couple and their friends soon accepted them as a pair except, that is, for

Elaine, who hadn't forgotten being singled out by Matthew in the first place and did her best to claim his attention. She was jealous of Nicola and showed it, but Nicola took no notice. After two weeks, she knew she was in love with Matt and felt sure that her feelings were returned by Matt though no words were said. She accepted his kisses and light-hearted love-making in the evenings they spent together but refused to sleep with him and this was the cause of their first quarrel.

The term had passed swiftly and as Christmas approached, everyone was throwing parties; in the end, Nicola decided that it was her turn and twelve of them squashed into her small attic room to the sounds of loud music and a plentiful supply of beer and cider but not a lot to eat. It was no different from any other party, there was a lot of laughter, some serious talk about their future plans and hopes and a final breaking up as couples paired up and drifted away.

Then only Nicola and Matt were left, with a room full of empty cans and bottles and crisp packets.

"Nicky," said Matt with an arm round her shoulder, he had called her Nicky from the start except when he was very serious. "I must help you clear up but give me a kiss first."

Nicky smiled up at him. "It's OK, Matt, it can be left until morning." And she put her arms round him and raised her face to his. Her lips parted under the force of his kiss and she felt a sudden urgency in his body which hadn't been there before. "Nicky, Nicky." He was breathing heavily. "You are so beautiful, I want you. Let me stay the night, Nicky."

Nicky stiffened instantly even while she felt she wanted to press closer. She knew that some of the other girls slept with their boyfriends but she had made up her mind from the start that she was not going to let herself get involved in a relationship with another student.

"Nicky?"

She pulled slowly away from him and she saw a bewildered look come into his face.

"No, Matt, I've got to say no, I'm not going to start anything like that."

He showed the first signs of anger at the same time trying to persuade her. "But, Nicky, you love me, I know you do. And you want me as much as I want you, there's nothing wrong in that."

She shook her head. "I'm sorry, Matt, yes I do love you very much but I made up my mind that I wouldn't sleep with anyone while I was at college and what I feel for you isn't going to change it."

He stared at her and his words were hard. "You're a little bitch. You had me thinking you were there for the asking and then you say no. I've got a good mind to make you do what I want."

"But you wouldn't, Matt, you're not like that."

11

Again he stared at her. "You're right, Nicola Greenhowe, you're too bloody right. But I know someone else who won't say no and I'm off there straight away. That's it between us, do you hear? I shan't come to college in the morning and the next day I'm going home. So it's goodbye, Nicky, and next term you can find another playmate."

He turned from her, grabbed his coat, stepped over the debris on the floor and was out of the room, slamming the door behind him.

Nicky didn't cry, she felt sad, she felt guilty, she had lost Matthew through her own pride. Slowly she picked up the cans and bottles and put them in a box; I shan't stop loving him, she said to herself, I know he's gone to Elaine. She's been panting for him. A tear trickled down her cheek, she dashed it away. I'm not going to cry for Matthew Hunter, I've come here to work and I'm going to work, nothing will stop me.

She didn't see Matthew again that

term, spent a miserable Christmas, then dreaded going back to college in January. But the term started and as she had expected, Matt was to be seen everywhere with a triumphant Elaine. Nicky threw herself into her work, missed Matt unbearably but somehow the heartbreak had increased her perceptive powers and she knew she was doing some good work. Perhaps we need adversity, she said to herself rather ruefully.

A sudden change came at the end of February on a bitterly cold day when they had been sent out to do some sketches at the shipbuilding yard. It was a fascinating scene with an activity, noise, smell and bustle peculiar to shipbuilding and if she hadn't been so cold, Nicky would have enjoyed it. She sat huddled in a duffel coat, wearing a thick, woolly hat and fingerless mitts, trying to forget the wind and to concentrate on her work.

"Nicky."

She looked up quickly, only Matt

called her name in just that way.

"Matt." She said only his name, she felt like asking where Elaine was but he was on his own and for some reason he had sought her out.

He sat down by her side. "Can I talk to you? You can say no if you like, I'll understand." He looked at her half-finished sketch. "That's good. You've been doing some good work, haven't you? I've noticed."

She glanced at him. She had never seen him so serious and yet she thought she had seen him in all moods. Had he broken up with Elaine? She was dying to ask but she thought she'd better leave it to him.

"I've missed you, Nicky."

"But . . . "

"Oh, I know what you are going to say, that I've had Elaine. And that's about it. I rushed to Elaine when you refused me and now I'm paying for it." He was frowning heavily.

"What do you mean, Matt?"

"Well, to put it crudely, Elaine's

fine in bed but that's about all she thinks about. You can't have a serious conversation with her, now she's having a fling with Johnny Vilven because she knows I'm fed up with her."

Nicky could sense what was coming. "And now you want to come back to me?"

"I can't ask you, can I?"

I'm a fool, she was saying to herself, I'm a damn fool but I still love him and I'd give anything to have our old friendly relationship back again.

"Matt, you know very well why we split up and I haven't changed my mind."

He took her hand and touched the tips of her cold fingers that were peeping through the woollen mitts. "Nicky, do you think we could go back to as we were before Christmas? I won't ask you for what you're not prepared to give. I was foolish, I realise now that sex isn't the be all and end all of a relationship. I miss our talks, the work we did together and I think

15

I work better if you're around. But I don't know about you, you've been working hard, haven't you? I admire your guts, you didn't let the quarrel upset your work, did you?"

"I tried not to," Nicky replied. "I did miss you, Matt, I still do miss you but I was determined not to let it affect my work. I even thought the split made me paint better than before. I couldn't really understand it."

"'Sweet are the uses of adversity'," he quoted.

Nicky laughed then. "Oh, Matt, you understand, we do understand each other, don't we? Shall we give it another try? I'm willing."

He put his hands on her shoulders and dropped a light kiss on her lips. "Bless you, Nicola Greenhowe, you're a brick. Now let's get down to some drawing or they'll be going off for a lunch break or something."

The next two months were happy ones. Matt went up to Hexham at half-term and Nicky was pleased to go to his home in Ripon for the Easter weekend. They all went to the cathedral on Easter Day.

The last term began and they were given their final big project to do; Nicky worked furiously. The friendship between Matt and Nicky progressed but was not so intense and she was happy and lived in the present. They did sometimes talk of the future and to Nicky it sometimes seemed to be a future that would always contain Matt even though they had to go their separate ways. He talked of marriage as a state he would like to enter into at some distant future day and Nicky knew that he was meaning a marriage to her.

There were only three weeks of term left when Matt dropped his bombshell. Their plans for the next year were made; Matt was going to Stirling University to read art history and Nicky was staying on at Newcastle for a second year, this time to concentrate on fine art. Most people had been for their interviews and had got places at various universities and colleges.

That week, Nicky had found Matt somewhat preoccupied but said nothing, putting it down to the pressures of the last few weeks of term. She was in her room just packing up her painting stuff when there was a furious knocking at the door quite late in the evening. Thinking it must be one of the other girls in the house, she called "Hallo."

The door opened and Matt stood there and for a moment she felt quite alarmed. He was sombre and brooding, his dark eyes even darker, his hair untidy, it was almost as though he had been drinking heavily.

"What is it, Matt? It's late for you to come round."

"I've got to see you." He stepped into the room and shut the door.

"Aren't you going to sit down?" she asked him.

"No."

Nicky almost trembled at the tense

syllable, this wasn't like Matt at all.

"Nicky, I should have come before. I've been putting it off all the week."

So there had been something wrong, she thought. "It sounds as though it's bad news, Matt. Has something happened at home?"

He shook his head. "I've been home but everything's all right, in fact they've been damn good to me."

Matt was talking in riddles, it was not like him to be unclear in what he was trying to say.

"Hadn't you better tell me, Matt, and for heaven's sake, sit down."

He suddenly collapsed into a chair and put his head in his hands; Nicky felt utterly bewildered.

"Matt."

He lifted his head and looked straight at her at last. "Nicky, I'm leaving college at the end of the week."

"Leaving college?" Her voice was a faint echo of his.

"Yes, I have to leave, you see, I'm getting married."

If he had thrown cold water in her face, Nicky could not have had more of a shock, she barely understood what he was saying.

"Getting married? But . . . who . . . "

"I'm marrying Elaine, you see she's going to have my baby, I have to marry her. We're going to live at Ripon and then she'll come to Stirling with me. I'm not giving that up, my parents are helping us out."

Nicky stared and stared at the Matt she had come to know so well, her thoughts chaotic. She had brought this on herself, she had refused him and he had turned to Elaine and now this was the result; but he didn't love Elaine, it would be a disaster yet he was doing the proper thing for the sake of the baby. What a mess, what an unholy mess.

"You're not saying anything, Nicky."

She was angry for a moment. "Well, what can I say? That I'm very pleased and that I hope you'll be very happy together? Well, I suppose I do hope that, but I happen to love you, Matthew Hunter, and I thought . . . I imagined you loved me too. You don't love Elaine, I know you don't."

"No, I don't love Elaine but it will probably work out all right. I'll have to make it work." He stopped abruptly and took her hand. "Nicky, will you let me say I'm sorry? I do love you, I know that now; but this is goodbye, I shan't see you again."

Nicky knew she was going to cry.

"Please go, Matt, go to your Elaine and for heaven's sake, stick to her."

"Nicky . . ."

"Please go, Matt."

He said no more but ran his hands through his hair, gave her one long look, turned and rushed out of the room.

Nicky did cry then, she thought she cried for hours and that her heart was broken. She knew that Matt was right and that she would never see him again and she lay in her bed and wept until she finally fell asleep.

The rest of that term was a nightmare but at least she didn't have to face Matthew or Elaine at college. She threw herself into her work and produced some brilliant paintings almost as though she could work best when at breaking point.

She got a job in Paris that summer and then spent another year at College. Gradually the memory of Matt faded and she didn't meet anyone else until she took a job with a small firm producing greetings cards on the outskirts of Alnwick. Nicky went for the interview and liked the owner-manager, John Normanby, very much; she also liked the set-up in the studio and accepted the job gladly. John was almost ten years older than she was, he was a competent artist and ran a successful business. After two years, they bought an adjoining property and opened a gallery mostly of Nicky's paintings but also some of John's. At the same time, they moved in together living in the flat above the new gallery. John had wanted to marry her but Nicky refused, she liked him but she knew she did not love him in the same way she had loved Matt and would not commit herself.

The small business prospered, they enlarged the gallery and took on more staff in the studio; then they moved into a cottage in the village but still Nicky refused to marry John; Matt was just a memory to her now but she knew she would never marry except for love. The years slipped by and when Nicky had just passed her thirtieth birthday, John met Sally and Nicky was to receive another upset in her life.

Sally was a young American girl who had come to work in the studio; she was small and dark and pretty and Nicky knew instantly that John had fallen in love with her. There was nearly a twenty years' age difference between John and Sally but it did not seem to matter for she felt the same for John and the two of them went about starry-eyed.

The outcome was that John sold the business to Nicky, married Sally and went over to America. Nicky stayed on her own in Alnwick for another year, then in a sudden impulsive mood which was out of character, she sold out to a businessman from Berwick who had been pressing her. She wanted to do only one thing and that was to buy her own studio in London and sell to the galleries there; she had the money, she was still young and if she didn't do it now she never would, she convinced herself.

So Nicky found her house, near the river in Chiswick, and had the attics converted to a studio with plenty of roof lights. Three weeks after settling in, she decided to go to her first gallery in the city and found herself staring across the crowded, colourful room at the opening of the Orion Gallery . . .

"Nicola, Nicola. Nicky, it must be you."

She returned from her reverie to the sound of Matt's voice and found herself looking once again into his deep, dark eyes.

2

"MATT."

It was all Nicky could say, she was speechless with an inner excitement but needn't have worried because Matt said it all for her.

"Nicola, fancy meeting you here, fancy meeting you today of all days. I didn't know you were in London, we lost touch, didn't we?"

Can he have forgotten why we lost touch, Nicky wondered, and she said the first thing that came into her head.

"Are you exhibiting a picture, Matt? I haven't seen it."

He looked at her with an odd expression on his face and then took both her hands in his and held them tightly. "Didn't you know, Nicky, isn't that why you've come? It's my gallery.

26

I'm the owner, my very first London gallery. You must have known."

Nicky was shaking her head and laughing up at him. "No, I've only just arrived in London and it's the Orion Gallery after all, it's not as though it's got your name."

It was Matt's turn to laugh. "I didn't want to call it the Matthew Hunter Gallery, but don't you see, Nicky? Orion was the Hunter of Greek mythology and the Orion Gallery sounds good, doesn't it?" Nicky felt she was being lifted high up in the air, it just couldn't, couldn't be true. But Matt was still speaking. "But, Nicky, you don't seem a day older and here am I going grey! You are as beautiful as ever . . ."

He broke off as lights flashed in front of them and they turned to find themselves surrounded by photographers and pressmen.

"Mr Hunter, keep holding her hands, just like that."

"Is she a girl friend, Mr Hunter?"

Matt was good-humoured and pulled a face at Nicky. "She's Nicola and she's a painter and we were at art school together."

"Is she an old flame, then, Mr Hunter?"

"You might say that." Matthew grinned and held on to Nicola's hands even more tightly. "That's all gentlemen, you've got the press release and there are a lot of people I must see. Nicky, we must meet, can you wait until the crush is over and come back after six o'clock? I can't stop and talk to you now."

"I'll have a look round now, Matt, then come back if you like. I'd like to see you, too." She said it almost shyly.

"Good girl, now I must go and find that *Guardian* critic, I'm relying on good reviews in the papers tomorrow."

"I think you'll get them, Matt, it's a great exhibition from what I've seen so far. I'll see you later, then."

Nicola left him and went from picture

to picture seeing neither shape nor colour in front of her, she saw only Matt's face and his eyes and his laughter. He hadn't changed, he just hadn't changed; oh, he was older and greyer and here he was with his own gallery just as he'd always dreamed about, but it was almost as though the years in between had never happened. And it was fifteen years, she said to herself, we were in our teens and now we are past thirty.

Then she remembered Elaine and looked around wondering if she was there, wondering even if they were still together. She left the gallery as soon as people started to drift away and when she got home, she sat and thought for a long time. I wonder if I should go back, she said to herself, it's not always a wise thing to try and put the clock back; it was uncanny in a way, meeting like that, it was almost as though it was yesterday. But I don't want to intrude on him and Elaine and they've probably had other children, too.

All the afternoon, she was hesitant and undecided and when six o'clock came, her nerve failed her. No, she thought, it was nice seeing him but that's it; that chapter is closed. And she set about getting a meal and trying to forget that tantalizing look of recognition and pleasure in Matt's eyes and the clasp of his hands around hers.

Half way through her meal, the phone rang. She got up puzzled as she knew very few people in London and her family rarely rang her up.

"Nicola?"

She couldn't mistake his voice.

"Matt, how on earth did you find me?"

She heard his laugh. "There's such a thing as directory enquiries even if I didn't have an address. I just had to keep my fingers crossed that you were still Greenhowe and that there wasn't more than one of you. I was lucky. Nicky, I'm still at the gallery, you didn't come back."

"I'm sorry, Matt, I wasn't sure."

"What do you mean, you weren't sure? That's not very explicit."

"I wasn't sure if you really wanted me to come or if it was said in the excitement of the moment and . . ." she hesitated.

"And, Nicky?"

"I wasn't sure if I wanted to put the clock back."

"It would be very nice to meet up again, Nicola." Matt spoke very slowly and seriously and she could but heed him.

"You really want to?" she asked.

"Yes, I do and Nicola, listen; your address is W4, it can't be all that far from us, we live just off Kew Green."

"I'm quite near the river in Chiswick, that's extraordinary, Matt."

She heard him chuckle. "It's fate, Nicky, fate playing into our hands. I'm leaving the gallery now, can I call and see you on the way home?"

The hesitation was still there. "Well, yes if you'd like to, I'll give you the directions. How long will you be?"

"About half an hour I should think, I've missed the rush hour so I shouldn't be held up. See you, Nicky."

Nicky put down the phone and found she was trembling. I'm not sure if I can cope with an exuberant Matt, she thought, he's obviously still on a high after the opening of the gallery. A sudden thought struck her. He had said 'we live' and 'us', it sounded as though he and Elaine were still together. And yet he hadn't been in a rush to get home, it was impossible to work it all out, she would just have to pull herself together and wait and see.

Matt's car pulled up outside her house in Lacey Street, Chiswick, exactly half an hour later. It was a road of tall Victorian houses, well kept and renovated and made for spacious family living. Nicky had turned the whole of her attic floor into a studio and was well pleased with her home. She greeted Matt at the door and took him through to the living-room at the back of the house; it had a patio window giving a green and peaceful view down a long back garden with tall trees in the distance. It was late spring, the sun was down but the evenings were light and the winter chills had gone from the air.

"This is nice," Matt said as he sat down.

Nicky offered him a drink but he gave a slight groan. "I've had sips from so many different drinks today, I shall be over the limit if I'm not careful. Could you manage coffee?"

Nicky brought in the coffee and they sat and looked at each other; it was almost as though the thoughts of both of them were back in the past.

Matt was the first to speak. "Nicky, I'm afraid I can't stay long this evening but I was anxious not to lose sight of you and I want to ask you if you would have dinner with me so that we can catch up on all our news."

Knowing she could not refuse, Nicky smiled at him and was glad to see the answering warm look in his eyes. "Yes, I would like that, Matt," she told him.

"Well, this week is going to be hectic with the opening of the gallery so I'll give you a ring next week and fix up an evening. Everything's gone so well today but I've got to wait for the critics' verdict in tomorrow's papers and I'm feeling shattered. In any case, I've got to pick up Gemma on my way home, I mustn't stop any longer."

"Who is Gemma?" Nicky asked curiously.

Matt looked as though he was surprised at her question. "She's my daughter, she goes to a friend to do her homework after school and stays there until I pick her up. So I hope you will excuse me, Nicky, I shall look forward to seeing you next week."

She didn't ask him any more questions even though she felt puzzled and she walked with him to the front door and saw him off, watching the big car disappear down the street, her mind in a whirl after all that had happened that day.

Going back into the house, she opened the patio door and stepped out into the garden. She thought perhaps a stroll in the cool quiet of the evening might quieten the turmoil of her brain and the excitement of her emotions.

The garden had been well designed for easy maintenance by the previous owner and Nicky was delighted with it as she was not a keen gardener. It was long and narrow and laid entirely to lawn but there was an abundance of trees and carefully chosen flowering shrubs which made it an oasis in a maze of London streets. There was a birch tree half way down the garden already showing its first delicate green and underneath it had been placed a wooden seat. Here Nicky sat quietly to think.

Her life, for many years, had been hard-working, happy and settled; living with John had been a smooth and easy experience for he had been a good companion and undemanding. When he had met Sally, Nicky hadn't been upset for she had never pretended to love him and she had been pleased for him that he and Sally were so happy. She had felt ready for a change in her life and had moved to London with great enthusiasm and great hopes.

Only occasionally had she thought of Matt, and then only in the sense that one would dearly love to know just what had happened in the life of someone who had been a first love. Deep emotions were something buried in the past and she had parted from John with no regrets and a resolve to come to London to concentrate on her painting and to get involved with no one.

And what had happened? Matthew Hunter had swept into her life again and she had to admit, as she sat in that quiet garden, one look at the handsome, charismatic Matthew and old memories had resurfaced and old feelings were giving her a sense of joy and wild surprise.

And she had said that she would see him again, too; already she knew she was looking forward to the occasion. For the second time, Matt was showing his ability to sweep her off her feet.

She frowned as she suddenly remembered his words abut Gemma, 'my' daughter he had called her. Did that imply that Elaine was no longer on the scene? What had happened to Matt in those intervening years? She would have to have patience, she would learn soon enough.

She was calmer when she went indoors but she could not deny that underneath the calm was a feeling of pleasure and anticipation at the thought of seeing Matt again. She wondered if he would keep his promise to ring her or whether it had been made when he was on a high of achievement and success.

Nicky was to hear from Matt sooner than she had expected for the phone rang not long after nine o'clock the next morning. She had been reading the review of the exhibition in the *Telegraph* and wished she had asked for Matt's number so that she could ring him up and congratulate him; the critic had been both complimentary and enthusiastic.

"Nicky!" There was laughter in the familiar voice.

"Matt, what is it?" She could not imagine why he should be ringing her at that hour.

"Have you seen the papers?" he asked her.

"Yes, there's a marvellous review in the *Telegraph*. I was just wishing I could ring you up to congratulate you. Are the others just as good?"

"Yes, they're fantastic. But it's not the heavies, it's the tabloids."

"The tabloids? They've not mentioned it, have they?"

Matt gave a chuckle. "Well, they have in a way."

"Matthew Hunter, what are you talking about?"

"Nicola, my dear girl, you've got your picture in the paper . . . "

"Me?" Nicola shrieked out. "What on earth have I got to do with it?"

"It's a gorgeous one of you, Nicky, holding my hands and looking at me as though you adored me!"

"Matt, stop laughing. You can't be serious." Nicky was appalled.

"I'm perfectly serious and you look beautiful, they say so, too."

"Oh, Matt, what an awful thing to happen; are you cross?"

"No, sweetheart, I'm not cross. It's all good publicity."

"Matt."

"Nicky, I must go, I have to be at the gallery. You go out and buy some papers and you'll see what I mean. See you next week, goodbye for now."

He had put his phone down without giving her the chance to say anything else. She pulled a face, I've certainly met up with Matthew Hunter again, I've a feeling life's never going to be the same again.

She hurried down the street to the newsagents in the row of shops in the next road. She bought one of each of the tabloids and dashed home again, she dare not look at them in the street.

Every single one carried the same story and Nicky ended up hooting with laughter, it was the only thing to do.

'Orion owner meets old flame'

'We were students together . . . ?'

'Painter sweethearts'

And the most outrageous of all.

'Old lovers meet at new gallery'

And there were the pictures; she and Matt holding hands and looking at each other as Matt had said; and in the one where she was facing the camera, she looked radiant. Oh, dear.

And the story was embellished of course, how they had been lovers at art school and then separated; and she had gone to the gallery to meet up with him again. Did it spell future romance?

Nothing about Elaine, Nicky noticed and no mention of Gemma; just the usual tabloid tittle-tattle and love of scandal and romance. Matt hadn't been upset by it and she wouldn't be either, there would be another such story tomorrow about other people.

So she tried to forget Matt and concentrated hard on her work.

She had plenty to do. Already she supplied two galleries in Sussex with watercolours in her own distinctive style. They were nearly all landscapes as Nicky had a love affair with green and with trees in particular; she also did portraits and had achieved great success with them in Northumberland. Her ambition was to stage her own show in a small gallery somewhere in London and she worked with this in mind. It occurred to her that it might not be a bad thing to know Matthew Hunter.

It was a week before she was to meet Matt again and he arrived in Lacey Street casually dressed and all prepared to take her to a small restaurant that was a favourite of his near Richmond

Common; it had the advantage of being near and quiet.

Nicky had chosen her clothes very carefully and knew she looked good in a printed, calf-length skirt worn with a top of cornflower blue; her hair was long and shiny and although she did not know it herself, she looked very little older than she had done when she and Matt had last met. A few lines on her face, perhaps, and a more mature and serious expression but in Matt's eyes she looked as beautiful as ever and he said so as he handed her into the car with old-fashioned gallantry.

"Nicola, I said it when I first saw you at the gallery and I'll say it again, you are as beautiful as ever and you don't look a day older."

"Flattery, Matt?" she smiled across at him.

"No, I really mean it. Did you get the papers, Nicky? Weren't they glorious? And very good of you, too."

Nicky gave a half-hearted groan. "I ended up by laughing at them, it was the only thing to do. They were obviously convinced that we were long lost lovers just meeting up again."

"We weren't, were we?" She could tell he was serious.

"No, Matt, good friends at one time but not lovers."

"I hope we can be good friends again, I've found you again and I'm determined not to lose you."

Conversation went on in this light-hearted vein until they reached the restaurant and were well into a very good meal.

Over coffee, Matt suddenly became serious. "Did you ever marry, Nicky? Tell me what happened to you."

So she told him about her venture in Alnwick and about John and then about her decision to come to London. "I want to try and get a show, Matt," she told him. "A one-woman exhibition, as it were."

"You always were ambitious, Nicky, it's not easy in London, you know. I'll have to come and have a look at your work, maybe I could put some at Orion to give you a start. But I'm not promising, it's got to be good. I've got high standards and I look for the more traditional stuff not what some of the art schools turn out these days. I know what people will buy and it's surprising how conservative the public are. Do you know that a Cezanne still life of apples on a plate went for $26 million this week?"

She nodded but smiled at the same time. "Yes, I saw it in the paper. But you're talking about Cezanne, Matt, and there are still a lot of Americans and Japanese around with plenty of money. The recession doesn't seem to have hit them as it has the European countries."

He looked at her. "Would you like me to see some of your stuff, Nicky? You must have been working hard if you've got a show in mind . . . "

"I'd love you to, Matt, but you might be disappointed. I seem to have got this thing about green and leaves and trees but it may be just a stage I'm going through."

"No, stick with it, Nicky, you must be instantly recognisable, you want people to be able to say 'Look that's a Nicola Greenhowe'. By the way, I'm glad you hadn't got married and changed your name or I'd never have found you. There was only one Greenhowe as it happened, useful to have an unusual name sometimes."

"I don't often get it spelt correctly though, the last 'e' usually gets left off."

They finished their coffee and Matt sat smiling at her. "Do you know what I'd like to do now, Nicky, it's not dark yet? Richmond Park is just around the corner, shall we go for a walk? I often go there when I've been stuck indoors all day."

Nicky stood up, she liked the idea. "It would be lovely, Matt, can I get my jacket from the car?"

"Yes, we'll walk there, they won't mind if we leave the car in the carpark,

I'll just go and tell them."

Five minutes later, they were in a different world. Wide open spaces and grass and trees as far as the eye could see. It was a fine, clear evening, the sun just disappearing behind the western fringes of the trees. They went into the park at Sheen Gate and walked across the meadow, past the quietly grazing deer and towards the shady woods on the hill to the south.

They walked silently at first and Nicky felt a strange contentment; Matt had taken her hand as though they were still students together and in the way that time can deceive, it was hard to believe that fifteen years had passed since they had last walked hand-in-hand.

Nicky was waiting for Matt to tell her about his personal life, about Elaine and about Gemma, but she listened in vain. He seemed determined to talk about anything except the things of the heart.

She asked him how the first week

at the gallery had gone and he was enthusiastic.

"Beyond expectations," he told her. "We've sold a lot and there are some good paintings coming in. Also I hope to do a Mark Taplin exhibition next month." Matt was speaking of one of the country's leading abstract artists.

"Mark Taplin? You've done well to get him," Nicky remarked.

"Yes, I got to know him in Edinburgh, I haven't told you, Nicky, that there is already one Orion Gallery. I opened a small gallery in Edinburgh soon after leaving Stirling. It's still doing well, I've got a good girl up there looking after it; Laura Macmillan, I met her at university, we were both reading art history."

She looked up at him curiously, he must be thinking of his years at Stirling and yet Elaine was still not mentioned. Nicky could hardly contain her curiosity.

"You've done very well, Matt," was all she said.

He laughed. "I had a one-track mind," he said. "And it was a good course at Stirling, I didn't change my mind about wanting to own a gallery. I got some premises at a very reasonable rent with living accommodation above, my first exhibition was all students' work from the university and it just took off. The Edinburgh gallery did well, then I came down to London to work at the Tate for the experience and now I've got the second Orion."

Nicky could contain herself no longer, if Matt rebuffed her, if she was prying, she just couldn't help it.

"Matt," she said with a slow query in her voice and he looked quickly down at her. "Matt, what happened to Elaine?"

3

MATT stopped. He turned to face Nicky and took both her hands in his. "I've been waiting for you to ask me that," he said. He looked around them and pointed to a seat under a group of trees. "It's a long story and not a happy one. Shall we sit down or will it be too cold for you?"

"No, I'm not cold, it's a nice evening," Nicky replied and they walked to the seat and sat down.

"Nicky, you've been very honest with me and I think I owe you the truth. It's hard to remember that the last time I was with you was the day before I left college to marry Elaine. Did you ever forgive me?"

Nicky looked into his eyes.

"I cried for a whole day and then I worked and I've never stopped working since. After a while, I began to forget what had happened and then the years just seemed to slip past." She paused. "It wasn't so easy for you, Matt?"

He shook his head. "No, it wasn't easy from the start. I know I didn't love Elaine but it was my child and I married Elaine for the child's sake. We started off living with my parents in Ripon but it didn't work; Mum and Dad were being very generous but they didn't take to Elaine. It wasn't surprising, she seemed to think that because she was my wife and was expecting a baby she had no need to work and she let Mum do everything. And Mum was still teaching, as you know. Then came the summer holidays and it was disastrous with us all in the house, so one day, when Elaine was out, I had a good talk with Mum and I agreed to take Elaine up to Stirling straight away and look for a summer job until the new term started. The baby was due at the end of September. It was a bit better after that; I got a job in a supermarket and Elaine stayed at home, she is lazy by nature and she didn't grumble . . . " he broke off. "Sorry, Nicky, I told you it was a long story."

"No, no," she reassured him. "I used to try and imagine how you were getting on so I'd like to know the truth."

"Elaine had a little girl and we called her Gemma. We had quite a nice flat, things were cheaper up there. I got on fine with my course and for a year things didn't work out too badly. Gemma was a good little baby and Elaine seemed happy enough. It was when Gemma got a bit older and began to run about and then to talk that the trouble started. Elaine had to give her more attention and seemed to resent it. Then when Gemma was nearly two, it all went wrong and it was partly my fault though I couldn't have guessed what was going to happen. It was a few weeks before the start of the new term. I used to go into the library on

51

the campus to do some work and I met an American artist, he was coming to lecture for a term on American art. He was about thirty and I got on fine with him, his name was Jay. Well, I started asking him back for a meal in the evenings after we'd got Gemma to bed. And you can guess what happened." Matt took her hand and looked at her ruefully.

Nicky could guess. "Elaine fell for him."

He gave a hard laugh.

"It wasn't difficult, was it? And Jay fell for her, too, you know what a pretty girl she was. They made no secret of it, he used to visit her at the flat if I was working late in the library. Well, to cut a long story short, at the end of that term, Elaine announced that she was going back to America with Jay and asked me for a divorce."

"But, Matt," Nicky broke in. "What about Gemma?"

"Elaine had lost interest in Gemma, the little girl was no more than a nuisance and an obstacle to her plans to go off with Jay."

"You mean . . . ?"

"Yes, she went off to America and left Gemma with me."

They were both silent, Nicky thinking with a shock of sickness of Elaine's callous behaviour and wondering how on earth Matt had managed.

"Whatever did you do, Matt?"

"I was determined to finish the year at university and get my degree. I took Gemma home for the Christmas holidays to ask Mum and Dad's advice and my dear mother said she would get leave of absence from school for two terms and would look after Gemma for me if I would make arrangements as soon as I was settled in a job after I'd got my degree." Matt looked down at the solemn Nicky. He had remembered something.

"Do you know what Mother said once, Nicky?"

She shook her head.

"She said to me that if I had to get

53

married while I was still at university, why couldn't it have been to that nice Nicola?"

Nicky grinned. "I liked your mother, Matt, she was very good to you."

"She spoiled me, I couldn't have managed without her, and Dad too, of course. They've been down to see the gallery, by the way."

"And you got a good degree?"

"Yes, I got a first, I don't know how I did it; you said it once, Nicky, about working better in adversity."

She nodded but was silent.

"I think it gives a greater determination to do well against all odds, otherwise you'd go under." Matt was thoughtful and silent for a moment. "But I'm not sure how I got through the next months. While Mum still had Gemma during the summer holidays, I got hold of the premises in Edinburgh and set up the gallery. I worked all hours for I had to take on some hotel work just to keep me going financially; then I had to decorate the flat above the gallery ready for Gemma. It was quite good accommodation but was very shabby. But I was able to furnish a small room specially for Gemma and we had a large living-room, a kitchen and a bathroom as well as a good sized bedroom for me. It was a Victorian building not unlike yours. The gallery was due to open in September and I had to have Gemma back at the same time; she was nearly three by this time."

"And you brought her up, Matt?"

"Yes, I brought her up; for some reason, she adored me. Perhaps it was because I loved her from the start, while to Elaine she was just an encumbrance. I'm not sure, all I know is that she's always been devoted to me and still is. But to go back to Edinburgh, I got her into a day nursery until she was old enough for nursery school and I looked after her in the evenings and at weekends. I didn't go out in the evening for years, you wouldn't have recognised me! But it all fitted in, the gallery did well and gave me an adequate living, I could arrange the opening times to fit round taking Gemma to and from school and on Saturdays, I paid a student to come and look after her. That worked out as well and it was good for Gemma to have some female company."

"But you had no female company, Matt."

He looked down at her. "Not to begin with, I wasn't bothered. I'd had enough of females with Elaine and I was too busy to bother. Then as Gemma got older and I did make one or two friends, I found that Gemma objected so it hasn't been too easy."

"But what about Elaine? Does she ever come over and see Gemma?"

He shook his head. "After the divorce, we lost touch, I was given custody of Gemma and I assumed Elaine married Jay. At first, she would send presents for Gemma at birthdays and Christmas but even that's stopped now. I don't even know where she lives."

"So Gemma hasn't got a mother?"

"No, she's fifteen now and I can see trouble ahead. I think it's a time when a girl needs a mother, don't you?"

Nicky nodded. "Yes, I suppose I do. But how do you manage, Matt, like tonight? Have you had to leave her on her own?"

"No, I'm very lucky, she has a friend, Sarah Ketch, who lives not far away and Mrs Ketch is such a kind person. Sarah is an only child and Mrs Ketch is always pleased to have Gemma to stay the night if I am out. Then I collect them both and take them to school in the morning. It makes it very easy for me and I like Gemma to have Sarah for a friend, it's good for her." He laughed suddenly. "So now you are up-to-date on my life history, young lady, and do you realise it's getting dark?"

Nicky laughed, too. "I'd hardly noticed; thank you for telling me all that's happened, Matt. It hasn't been a happy time for you and you've done so well. I admire you."

"You used to say you loved me, Nicola."

"Matt, you know very well how old we were then, I think we are past love now."

"Speak for yourself, old lady of thirty-three, and come on, we'd better hurry back across the park before it really does get dark. You are getting cold, too."

They laughingly ran back to the car and were soon back in Lacey Street. Matt stopped the car and leaned over to take Nicky's hand in his. "Am I allowed to kiss you on the cheek to say thank you for a lovely evening?"

She felt his lips fleetingly touch her cheek and almost shivered at the soft contact. But she spoke with sincerity. "I've enjoyed it too, Matt, thank you very much."

"And you will let me come and see your work? One day next week perhaps? I'll give you a ring. Goodbye, Nicky."

She made herself more coffee when she got indoors, there was a lot of thinking to do. Matt's story had stirred her and she felt a genuine wish to meet the solitary Gemma. Perhaps she would one day.

Nicky thought about Matt a lot during the next few days. Although on the surface her routine of work wasn't disturbed, there was an inner turbulence she could not ignore. She knew it came from her meeting up with Matt again, his dominating good looks, his disturbing presence and touch and not the least the story of his break up with Elaine and the way he was devoted to Gemma. Her thoughts and feelings made her paint with a ferocity that had been lacking in her work for a long time and she knew she was painting well; at the same time, she wondered if Matt would consider it good enough to hang in the Orion Gallery. She knew she could accept and trust his judgement.

When she didn't hear from him, she was disappointed. Then as the days went by and there was still no word she began to wonder if she had imagined his enthusiasm, his infectious joy at meeting her again, and his promise to come and see her paintings. Saturday of the following week came and Nicky was sad and despondent and she knew that once again she had fallen under Matthew Hunter's spell. I can't fall in love with him again, she said to herself, I'm not a teenager any more and I refuse to admit to teenage feelings. I've been thinking about him far too much and reading too much into his behaviour, now I've got to forget him and get on with my life.

But when the phone rang on Sunday morning early and she knew it was him, her heart danced and she called herself a fool as she hurried to answer it.

"Nicky, please forgive me," were his first words.

"What is it, Matt?"

"We had a crisis at the Edinburgh Orion and I had to rush up there unexpectedly. Then while I was there I went round and did some buying and didn't get back till late last night. Did you think I had forgotten you?"

"Yes," she said bluntly.

His laughter came over the phone. "Oh, Nicola, you care, that's wonderful," he said and Nicky was cross with herself for giving away her feelings. But she listened to what he was saying with great pleasure.

"Can I come and see you this afternoon, Nicky? Gemma's gone out for the day with the Ketches. Would that be convenient?"

"Yes, I'd love to see you, Matt; would you like to come to lunch?" she offered suddenly.

"Bless you, I'd love to."

"It will have to be salad, it's all I've got in."

"Fine, I'll come about twelve o'clock. Is that OK?"

"Yes, we can have a drink before lunch then. See you later."

"Goodbye, Nicky."

Nicky banged down the phone. I'm crazy, she cried out loud, absolutely

61

crazy. I'm as excited as an eighteen-year-old and I can't wait to see him. Oh, Matt, you haven't changed.

He came bounding up the steps of Lacey Street house at twelve o'clock and his looks would have turned most heads. He was dressed in pale slacks and a loose sweater of dark chocolate brown with a cream design. He was all smiles and Nicky was pleased to see him; he confused her straight away by bending down and kissing her full on the lips as though it was the most natural thing in the world.

He told her about the Edinburgh trip while they had a drink and Nicky learned a little about the Scottish Laura at the gallery.

"She's having trouble with her two children, both boys," Matt was saying. "We have a lot in common, Laura and I. I told you we met at university and she got married when she was young, too, and it was a disaster. She was left with two boys to bring up and was thrilled to bits when I offered her the job in the gallery with the flat above. She's done very well but every so often one of the boys gets into trouble with the police and she has to appear in court. It's usually petty theft or shop-lifting or something like that, nothing violent, but it makes life difficult for Laura."

"How old are the boys?" Nicky asked.

"One is ten and one is twelve, they are nice boys but need a father." He grinned at her. "I like Laura very much and did offer to marry her then we could bring up Stuart and Ian and Gemma together; I thought it seemed a sensible idea. Gemma needed a mother and who better than Laura?"

"And wasn't it?"

Matt was solemn. "Nicky, I'd do anything to provide a mother for Gemma but I'm afraid that the young lady has different ideas. Laura and I gave it a try before committing ourselves to marriage. It was a fiasco. Gemma wouldn't speak to Laura, the boys hated Gemma and one of them started missing school and they also hated having a father. They behaved abominably so we gave up the idea and I brought Gemma down to London. But I still care what happens to Laura and give her all the support I can."

Nicky felt a pang which she knew was an absurd jealousy. He still cares for Laura, perhaps he will marry her when the children are older and more reasonable. But what does it matter to me? I'm settled in a career, I've only just met Matt again, it can't make any difference to me if he marries Laura or not. But suddenly and acutely and without warning, she knew that it did matter.

She jumped up quickly, gave Matt the Sunday paper and said that she would go and prepare lunch. She hardly remembered getting the meal ready but in no time, she was sitting opposite Matt, drinking wine and eating a quiche, hastily rescued from the freezer and heated in the microwave, and a good green salad with rice.

They washed up together, Matt insisted, and any onlooker would have thought the scene in the kitchen a happy domestic affair between a man and his wife.

When it got nearer the time to take Matt up to her studio, Nicky began to feel nervous. She longed to show Matt her paintings and yet at the same time she dreaded the moment. Matt wasn't going to let her delay.

"What about these paintings of yours, Nicky? I'm looking forward to seeing them."

"The studio is in the attic," she faltered.

"Lead the way."

The stairs up to the attic were narrow and uncarpeted and their steps sounded loud on the wooden boards. Neither of them spoke and when Nicky opened the door and they stepped inside the studio, they were still silent.

It was an enormous space with sloping ceiling at the back and front;

there were no windows but Nicky had put in two skylights which she thought made the light perfect. Against the walls, propped up against tables and chairs, lying in piles in the corners, were the paintings; at one end of the room there was a heap of frames and on an adjacent table, all the tools required by the picture framer.

Stupidly, Nicky pointed to the frames. "I do all my own framing, I went on a course. I think a painting can be ruined by the wrong frame."

She needn't have spoken. Matt was walking about; he went through a pile of canvases, he opened a large portfolio of water-colours, he looked at every single picture standing against the walls and he didn't say a word. Nicky's heart sank, she couldn't speak either. He doesn't like them and he doesn't know how to tell me; they were all right up in Alnwick but just not good enough for London.

When he turned to her and saw the usually buoyant Nicola looking sad and crestfallen, he knew what she was thinking and stood before her to look down into the bright blue eyes.

Nicky gasped when she met Matt's eyes for his expression could only have been one of excitement. She stared at him and didn't move when he put his hands out and clasped her round the waist. Nor did she move away when he pulled her closer and bent his head towards hers; he kissed her with a longing and a passion which seemed to echo his emotion on seeing her pictures, and Nicky returned his kiss without even understanding what was happening.

"Nicky," he whispered, "I couldn't tell you how I felt, I could only show you, that was how your paintings touched my feelings. Nicky, I'm an old hand at this business but once in a while you come across an artist whose work reaches out to you, it almost hits you in the stomach. And your reaction is physical, sometimes you feel you want to shout out loud. I felt I wanted to kiss you."

She gazed at him. "You mean you like them?"

"Magic, Nicola Greenhowe, sheer magic. Not a poor one amongst them. And that distinctive voice that is only yours, the greens, the colour of the leaves, the shapes of the trees." He pointed to the one that was in the front of the pile that stood by the table. "Look at the farm buildings, the roof of the farmhouse, central to the picture but secondary to the trees. They live, don't they, Nicola? They live for you."

"Yes," she replied quietly. "I suppose they do. I've never been away from trees or from the countryside except for the years in Newcastle. Now I've come to London and I wonder if I shall want to escape back to the trees again."

"No," he said. "It's an inner vision." He was still holding her close and his lips found hers again drawing a response from Nicky that she was not sure she was ready to give. "If you can go on painting like that, we can do a lot together, Nicky."

"What do you mean?"

He gave her a quick hug and then walked round the studio again; he carefully chose three pictures. "If you'll let me, I'll take these and show them at Orion, then we'll try some others slightly different. We'll sell them, Nicky, I know we will. You can trust my instinct. And then in a few months' time, I'll get a friend of mine with a smaller gallery to give you an exhibition of your own."

"Matt, don't go so fast. Are you sure you are right?"

"You are being insulting, Miss Greenhowe."

She could sense that he was laughing at her and the tense moments were eased. "I'm sorry, Matt, it's just that I can't believe it. You see, I know they did well in Alnwick but a small country gallery in the north of England is vastly different from a London gallery. You know that as well as I do."

"I do know it," he said seriously. "And I also know that these paintings of yours will do very well in London. You mustn't forget, Nicola, that I knew you had the talent all those years ago but I didn't know how it was going to develop. But I can see you've worked hard and well and you deserve a lot of success." Then he asked suddenly: "You are still working, aren't you?"

"Oh, yes, all the time. I send to two galleries in Sussex, they've taken my stuff right from the start and it's always done well."

He came and stood beside her still holding the paintings. "There you are, so you shouldn't be surprised. Will you let me take them today? They can be hung tomorrow."

It came home to her that he really was serious and all she could do was to thank him.

"Thank you very much, Matt. It's giving me the start that I was going to find so difficult. I was going to have to take one or two paintings into the galleries I thought might be interested. Now I'm getting in through the back door. I really am grateful to you."

They made their way downstairs and Matt seemed to want and sit and chat again so Nicky made the coffee they hadn't had after lunch.

"Where do we go from here, Nicky?" he suddenly asked her enigmatically.

"Whatever do you mean, Matt?"

He leaned across and took her hands in his with a touch that never failed to thrill and disturb her.

"Well, we've met again and we've got our business priorities sorted out, but would you like to go on seeing me socially, will you come out with me from time to time? I'm not suggesting a romantic involvement, I'm past all that kind of thing, but I would very much like your friendship, Nicky."

Nicky's state of mind was such that she felt that she would have followed him to the ends of the earth, but she replied very quietly and simply.

"I would like that very much, Matt."

"Good, I would like to ask you to my home. Would you like to come and meet Gemma, Nicky?"

4

NICKY'S reaction to Matt's question shocked her. He had said only a few days ago that he would do anything to provide Gemma with a mother; was he thinking of her as a suitable candidate? It seemed he was prepared to marry without love simply to have someone who would be able to cope with a difficult teenage daughter.

She knew she was silent for a long time and wasn't surprised when Matt followed up his question with another.

"What are you thinking about, Nicky? You look very solemn."

She raised her head and met the query in his eyes. "I was wondering if Gemma would want to meet me."

"Why should you say such a thing when you've not even seen her?" he answered.

"I was just thinking that perhaps

every female you introduce into the house she sees as a prospective mother, an intrusion into her own domain. I should think she's bound to feel resentful, and rather protective towards you too."

Matt gave a half groan. "You are too perceptive, Nicky. I'm afraid she doesn't behave very well. But I thought she might respond differently to you if she knew we had been students together."

Nicky had a sudden thought. "Is Gemma artistic, Matt? Has she inherited your talent, and Elaine's of course?"

He shook his head. "No, it's completely passed her by; all she thinks about is animals, she has done ever since she's been little and it hasn't been easy. We've got a cat but it's difficult to have a dog when we are out of the house so much. Fortunately her friend, Sarah, has got two dogs so the two girls spend a lot of time exercising the dogs on the common. I really think Gemma hopes to be a vet, she's chosen all the scientific subjects she was allowed for her GCSE's."

"It's a good career for a girl, Matt."

"Oh, I'm not opposed to it, I suppose I'd do anything that would make her happy."

She looked at him. "You feel guilty, Matt."

He nodded. "I suppose so, it doesn't seem right for a girl to grow up without a mother. Sometimes I feel very inadequate."

"I think it is better than growing up with parents who are at odds all the time." Nicky felt she needed to try and help Matt but found it hard to say the right things.

Matt seemed to think otherwise. "You sound as though you speak from experience, Nicky, and yet you have never married or had children of your own."

"I've seen what's happened to friends with marital problems, the children always seem to come off badly."

"Yes, you are right, look at Laura."

"Look at Laura," she echoed and she thought that Matt looked sad and thoughtful. Then she added quickly to change the subject. "But I would like to meet Gemma; when would you like me to come?"

He brightened visibly. "Next Saturday?" he suggested. "It's the first day we will both be at home."

"Yes, that will be fine."

"I'll draw you a little map to find us though it's not too difficult from here. It's marvellous having you near, Nicky."

She saw him off and then went straight up to the studio and made herself settle to work. She looked round her and remembered that Matt had been there, she also remembered his kiss. It had been so spontaneous and natural and she knew that the sensation of it had affected her deeply, and that she was very near to falling in love with him all over again.

That week, Nicky found that she was able to work well and took advantage of the light mornings and evenings that came as May advanced. She heard from Matt inviting her to go and see her pictures at the Orion Gallery and she took an afternoon off to go and do so. It gave her a great sense of achievement to see them hanging there and by the end of the week she learned that two had been sold, and please, said Matt, would she bring two more when she came on Saturday?

Nicky had no difficulty in finding No 2 Malton Square in Kew; she followed Matt's directions and found herself turning into a handsome square of dignified Regency buildings with trees and shrubs enclosed behind iron railings at its centre. She thought it was an unusually sober setting for the flamboyant Matt but when she got inside the house, she could see why it had attracted him. Matt greeted her with a quick kiss on the cheek and took the paintings from her, she followed him into the narrow hall and realised that the girl standing there must have seen the chaste salute.

Matt turned to Nicky and made the introductions. "Nicky, this is Gemma."

It was a sullen-faced girl with whom she shook hands and Nicky could hardly believe that this was Matt's daughter. Gemma was quite short and what Nicky would rather rudely have called dumpy, her hair was a nondescript brown hanging limply to her shoulders; only her eyes gave her away, the dark brown of Matt's and at that moment burning with resentment.

"Gemma, take Nicky into the living-room and I'll take the pictures up to the studio."

Nicky followed the girl into a beautiful room with high moulded ceilings, thick carpet and for the most part, furniture that matched the age of the house. Long velvet curtains hung at the windows that looked out over the square and the walls were covered with paintings of every conceivable period and style.

"Oh, what a lovely room," exclaimed Nicky.

No notice was taken of this remark by Gemma who launched into a surprising tirade against Nicky.

"You were the one who was holding hands with Dad in that newspaper picture; it said you were an old flame and another one said you were lovers; and I saw him kiss you when you arrived just now."

Nicky drew a deep breath, it was going to be even more difficult than she had imagined. Truth seemed to be the only recourse.

"Gemma, I knew your father when I was not much older than you are now. We were very great friends, but we weren't lovers. In fact, Matthew left me to get married to your mother."

"I haven't got a mother."

Nicky's heart plummeted, she had said the wrong thing straight away. Had she better try gentleness? She was wishing that Matt would come back.

"Don't you hear from her, Gemma?"

79

she asked as quietly as she could.

The girl shook her head vehemently. "No, not ever. She used to send me presents from America for my birthday and Christmas, they were great, she sent some fantastic things; but I don't get them any more. I think she's just forgotten me." She looked defiantly at Nicky. "I don't care though, I've got Dad, I don't need anyone else. I certainly don't need a new mother like he seems to think, we're OK as we are."

I've got into deep water very quickly, thought Nicky, whatever can I say next? But she was saved from thinking of anything by the arrival of Matt. He glanced from one to the other and looked rather grim; he could sense the tension that was already there between the two people he had wanted to meet each other.

"Let's go into the kitchen and have some coffee." he said.

Gemma looked at him. "I've got loads of homework, Dad, and I expect you and . . . you and Nicky want to talk." Without saying anything more to Nicky, she rushed out of the room and they heard her footsteps running up the stairs.

Matt took Nicky's arm and led her through to an enormous living kitchen that looked out over a long back garden rather like her own.

"Not a good start, Nicky?" he said.

She looked distressed. "I'm sorry, Matt, I just didn't seem to say the right things. I was trying to think of some way of soothing things over when you returned."

"At least she spoke to you, she never said a word to Laura though that was five years ago; but don't let it worry you, Nicky, I'm used to it. I've brought other friends home and they've all had a cool reception. I'm at my wits end really, I can see myself having a problem teenager on my hands if I'm not careful."

Nicky looked at him seriously. "She thinks so much of you, Matt, I don't think she would do anything to upset you deliberately."

"Not unless I did something to upset her," was his rejoinder.

"Like getting married again." Nicky felt she was being brutal.

"You've said it, Nicky; if only I could find someone that I liked and who Gemma liked too."

"Am I in the running then, Matt?" She didn't know why she said it, the words just seemed to slip out.

He put out a hand and laid it over the top of hers. "Oh, Nicky, don't say it like that, so sarcastically. We've only just met up again and I just want to get to know you. Don't you feel the same? Please say you do."

She couldn't help smiling. "Yes, I do, Matt."

He moved his hand away with a sigh of relief. "Don't worry about Gemma, I just hope she will get used to you being on the scene and will stop being too hostile. I think she's terrified that

I'll start loving someone else and stop loving her."

"It's understandable, Matt, you are all she's got."

"You do understand, bless you, we'll take it slowly."

He got up and Nicky followed him to the kitchen window and they both looked down the long garden. There were beds of wallflowers and forget-me-nots and the bright yellow splash of a large potentilla. Lilac trees were in full bloom and the garden looked very colourful.

"You like colour in your garden, Matt," Nicky said. "Not like me with all my greens."

He smiled and looked down at her. "No, I actually like gardening and grow all my annuals from seed myself. It will soon be time for planting out the alyssum and French marigolds, tagetes too, I love their bright gold that lasts all the autumn. Come on let's have a walk down the garden, then we'll think about lunch."

"I didn't think I was staying for lunch."

"Of course you are, Gemma will get it ready; she's a good cook though we do take it in turns."

They talked painting and pictures after that and Nicky was fascinated to hear of Matt's week in the gallery. He was very pleased with things and Nicky liked to listen to him.

Over lunch, things were a little easier. Gemma had cooked a nice chicken risotto and Nicky was appreciative; they had wine and Gemma seemed more on equal terms with her elders. Nicky heaved a sigh of relief and offered to do the washing up; Gemma helped her while Matt pottered in the garden.

Nicky took the plunge and felt immediately that she had said the right thing. "Have you got a cat, Gemma?"

"Yes, he's probably after the baby birds at the bottom of the garden."

"Oh, Gemma, how can cats be so gorgeous and yet so cruel at the same time?"

There was a silence and Nicky waited.

Then the words came out with a rush and it was the first time that Gemma had spoken without the note of hostility in her voice. "Do you like cats, Nicky? Have you got one?"

"Yes, I love them but I haven't got one at the moment. I had a cat in Northumberland but I'm afraid she had to be put down just before I moved to London. I haven't really thought of getting another one yet."

"What was wrong with her?"

Nicky glanced at the rather plain face that suddenly showed a previously hidden intelligence and interest.

"It was sad really, her name was Topsy Two, we'd had a cat called Topsy when I lived at home with my parents, so when I got one of my own I wasn't very original and called her Topsy Two."

"I think that's nice. Was she ill?"

"Well, she wasn't really ill, she was only seven years old. I'd had her

85

neutered when she was a kitten and after a few years, a lump appeared where she'd had the op."

"Was it cancer?" Gemma was alive with interest and Nicky was amused at the change in her.

"Well, the vet said so and said he couldn't operate and that it would be kinder to have her put down. It broke my heart and I said I'd never have another one but now I'm in my own house with a lovely long garden, I think I might change my mind."

Gemma was quiet and Nicky thought they had exhausted what had been quite a long conversation.

"I want to be a vet."

Nicky looked down at her. "It's a lot of hard work, Gemma. Are you doing all the sciences?"

"Yes, I am, Dad doesn't mind. He knows I'll never be an artist like he is."

"It's a good career if you are prepared to work," said Nicky.

"Well, you have to work hard to do

86

anything worthwhile, don't you? I bet you've had to work hard to get those pictures of yours hung in Dad's gallery. He only has the very best, you know. You must be good."

Nicky was keeping her fingers crossed, things were taking a turn for the better, but she spoke quietly. "Yes, I seem to work all hours, especially when the days are long and light as they are at the moment."

They both turned at the click of the door to find Matt standing in front of them.

"Dad," Gemma cried out. "Nicky wants to have a cat now that she's settled in her London house. She had one before but it had to be put down."

Matt looked at her and then he looked at Nicky. A weight seemed to drop from him as though a miracle had happened; he smiled at them both.

"Barney is down under the lilac tree if you want to show him to Nicky, Gemma. But you'll have to hurry or he'll be off after the birds again."

He watched as the tall, fair-haired girl who was becoming so familiar again followed his plain, little daughter down the garden. "God bless her," he said under his breath and knew it was the older of the two he was referring to.

Not long afterwards, Nicky made her excuses to go home to work and Matt took her out to her car.

"Thank you for coming, Nicky. You are either very kind or very clever."

She looked at him in some surprise for it was a veiled remark. "What do you mean, Matt?"

"You got Gemma on to animals. It was the way to her heart and you knew it. Are you thinking it's the way to my heart, too?"

"Matthew Hunter," she said indignantly. "Don't be so arrogant. I like Gemma and I wanted to find something we could both talk about or it would have been most uncomfortable. Fortunately, my cat being ill really worked!"

He smiled. "Don't take any notice of me, Nicky, it's the embittered male in me." He put a hand on her shoulder. "I'll let you know how your paintings do and hope to see you next week sometime. Shall we have dinner again?"

"Thanks, Matt, it would be lovely. And thank you for today."

"Goodbye, Nicky."

When Matt went back indoors, it was to find Gemma waiting for him in the kitchen. "Did you like Nicky?" he asked her.

"She was all right, better than some of them you have brought home."

"Gemma!"

"Well, Dad, you know what I mean. But Nicky did tell me about her cat. Most of them are only interested in hearing about you. Are you in love with her, Dad?"

Matt sighed, and he had thought it had all gone so well. "No, I'm not, she's just a good friend."

"Well, I don't want her for a mother though I don't mind helping her to find a cat if she wants one. Is she coming next week?"

He looked at Gemma. How was he going to get through these next difficult years? But at least Nicky seems to have made a good impression, he said to himself.

"Yes, Gemma, I hope so."

It was to be less than a week before Nicky saw father and daughter again and it was all due to her thoughts about getting another cat. What Nicky had said to Gemma about the cat had not been just for conversational purposes. She had always been a cat-lover and once she had settled in Lacey Street, she found that she missed having a cat about the place. On the Wednesday of the following week, Nicky was in the newsagent's at the end of the road to pay her paper bill and on the way out she stopped and looked at the advertisements printed on cards in the window. They were always a fascination. Immediately one caught her eye.

GOOD HOMES WANTED FOR TABBY KITTENS
PHONE 994 3216
AFTERNOONS OR EVENINGS

Here's my chance, she said to herself as she walked home having made a note of the number. I've always had tabbies, I'll ring up this afternoon. And she found herself thinking of Gemma. I wonder if she'd like to come with me to see them and help me to choose one, she pondered. Matt will say I've got an ulterior motive but I shan't take any notice; if I'm going to see Matt at all then it would be nice if I got on well with Gemma.

She made arrangements to see the kittens in the evening, set her heart on having one and rushed out and bought some cat litter and a tray and some tins of food. Then after her evening meal, she kept ringing Matt's number until she got a reply.

"Matt, it's Nicky, is Gemma there?"

"Gemma?" There was great surprise in his voice. "You want to speak to

Gemma? Not to me?"

"Yes, please, I particularly want to speak to Gemma."

"I'll call her."

She waited a long time and wondered if Gemma was refusing to come to the phone. Then she heard the girl's voice, out of breath and on the defensive.

"Dad says you want to speak to me, I was doing my homework."

"Gemma, I've heard about some kittens and I'm going to see them tonight, would you like to come and help me to choose one? What about your homework?"

"Oh, Nicky." The name slipped out spontaneously. "That would be great. I haven't got a lot of homework, I can do it later on."

"Good, I'll pick you up in half-an-hour then."

They found the kittens in a small cottage down by the river. The owners of the cat were a young couple and the kittens had been well cared for and were house trained. There had been six in the litter but one had already gone which left four toms and one female to choose from; they were tumbling playfully in and out of the basket.

Gemma was in a seventh heaven. "Oh, I wish I could have one but I've already got Barney and Dad would never let me have two cats."

Nicky was amused. "Never mind, Gemma, are you going to help me to choose one?"

It wasn't difficult. Nicky didn't really want a tom and the female was the smallest and the most appealing. They all had lovely markings.

They had brought a shoe box lined with woolly material and Nicky let Gemma have charge of it and carry the kitten to the car. They were home in ten minutes.

"Are you going to keep her in the kitchen, Nicky?" Gemma asked when they got inside the house.

"Yes, I think so, then it's easier to sweep up any spills from the litter box. Put her in this corner by the boiler,

Gemma, it will be warm here."

The kitten was soon out of the box and exploring, she didn't seem frightened of being on her own and Gemma loved talking to her.

"What are you going to call her, Nicky? Will it be Topsy Three?"

Nicky shook her head. "No, I don't think so, it's a bit of a mouthful and I think I'd better start afresh. Would you like to give her a name, Gemma?"

Gemma looked up with delight. "Can I really? I'll have to think. My second name is Louise but that's not really suitable for a cat. I did have a hamster once called Millie but she died. Do you think we could call her Millie? It's short for Millicent," she added.

Nicky agreed and Millie the kitten became. When she fell asleep in her box, Gemma went over to her and pulled something out of her pocket.

"What's that, Gemma?" Nicky asked.

"It's a small, furry bear I got from my bedroom when I went to fetch my jacket. Millie's used to having the warmth of her mother and the other kittens, I thought it would be company for her."

Nicky looked at the young girl looking so seriously at the little scrap of a kitten. This was a different Gemma. And she wondered if in future Gemma would accept her more readily.

"Come on, Gemma," Nicky said. "I'd better take you home while Millie's asleep. You've still got your homework to do."

Gemma smiled as she stood up and spoke almost shyly and very politely. "Thank you for asking me, Nicky, it was very kind of you."

"It was very kind of you to come at a moment's notice, you must come over sometimes and see how Millie is getting on." Nicky looked at the girl cautiously wondering if she had said the right thing, but she got a cheerful reply.

"Yes, I'd love to."

They made their way quickly home to Malton Square and as Nicky had made no arrangements to see Matt, she just dropped Gemma, said goodbye and drove home again, anxious to make sure that Millie was all right. She let herself into the house and crept quietly into the kitchen, and at the same time there was a knock on the front door.

Frowning, she hurried to open it.

Matt stood there, his eyes both indignant and laughing. "What's all this about Millie? Have I been forgotten?" he asked.

5

FROM the direction of the kitchen could be heard a plaintive mewing. Nicky looked at Matt. "Listen," she said, and he came in and crept up the passage way.

He laughed out loud. "It's Millie. Gemma came bursting in full of this kitten called Millie and when I came out to speak to you, you'd gone. So I came straight over and almost beat you to it. I refuse to be supplanted by a kitten called Millie. Let me see the wretched animal then!"

Nicky, who was laughing too, opened the kitchen door and found Millie still in her box, quite all right and obviously crying for attention. She picked up the little scrap and handed her over to Matt who cradled her in his long hands. Nicky liked the expression on his face.

"Take her into the living-room and nurse her while I get drinks," she said. "Will you have whisky?"

"I'd rather have a beer if you've got one."

They sat over their drinks and watched Millie explore the room. Matt was thoughtful.

"You asked Gemma to go with you to choose the kitten," he said at last.

"Yes, I thought she would like that."

"She did like it, she was full of it, Nicky. It was very kind of you, I've not seen her so animated for a long time." He lapsed into silence and Nicky knew what he was thinking.

"It's all right, Matt," she said. "It wasn't just a clever ploy to capture Gemma's affections. I like your daughter and I've told her she can come over and see Millie whenever she likes."

He got up suddenly, the kitten was trying to climb up his trouser legs. "Nicola Greenhowe, give that damned animal some milk and put it in its box.

I want to kiss you."

"Matt!"

But it was no good protesting for he had walked into the kitchen carefully holding Millie, had found the milk bottle and was pouring milk into the saucer that Nicky had put down. Then, as though she was the model of obedience, Millie let Nicky put her in her box where she immediately fell fast asleep.

"Oh, Matt!"

The exclamation came from Nicky as she straightened up from bending over the kitten and Matt took her in his arms.

"Are you going to be as kind to me as you are to that cat?" he asked, looking deeply into her eyes.

Nicky's heart was beating fast and her whole body pulsed with the sensation of his nearness. His mouth sought the swell of her breast at the opening of her dress and she gave a gasp. Then he was kissing her and his lips were letting her know his desire and Nicky felt herself lost.

"Nicky," he whispered. "Can we go upstairs?"

She heard the question and did not at first take it in, his mouth was roaming her face and his hands were on her body. Then as his meaning became clear to her, she knew with a frightening force that she wanted him as much as he wanted her.

But no, she said to herself. Matt meant more to her than just a casual encounter and in that still, emotional throbbing moment, she knew that she loved him again; it was more than that, it was almost as though she had never stopped loving him. And it was love she wanted from him not just passion.

"Nicky," his voice was urgent. "Did you hear what I said?"

"Yes, Matt, I heard."

"Well?"

"Matt, don't ask me. I know I'm not an innocent young girl any more but I've just broken up one relationship

100

and I don't feel like starting another. In fact, I'm determined not to, my work is going to come first from now on."

He sighed resignedly. "I might have known you'd refuse me, I suppose it's marriage you are after. I've got a good mind to ask you to marry me for Gemma's sake, the girl's getting to like you."

"Matthew Hunter, you are infuriating, and I might as well tell you that I'll never marry without love."

"It's all right, Nicky, I wouldn't either, one loveless marriage is enough in anyone's lifetime. It's all your fault for looking so gorgeous with that damned kitten; you really care for it and you've only had it an hour! I wish you'd look at me like that."

Nicky laughed out loud. "Anything less like a kitten than you is hard to imagine. Matt, don't let's fall out over it. We've only just met again and I'd like to be friends, you told me yourself that you don't want to get romantically involved so we both feel the same."

"You are right, my love, and I'll just curb my passions. I've had enough practice, God knows."

What a strange life he has had, Nicky thought, tucking her arm through his, a disastrous marriage and then a small child to bring up. He must have had some girl friend somewhere along the line, a man like Matt; perhaps it was the capable Laura in Edinburgh. But it's going to be hard not to show him that I love him, she said to herself; I suppose if he ever came to love me then I would marry him and hope for the best with Gemma, but that's not now; Matt's love would be worth waiting for.

During that summer, they saw each other regularly; Nicky's paintings did very well and Matt told her they were beginning to be sought after. It was time to be thinking about an exhibition and he had a small gallery in mind.

Nicky also saw quite a lot of Gemma; towards the end of term, exams over, she had more time and took to going over to Lacey Street to see Millie who wasn't going to be a small kitten for much longer. Nicky was pleased that Gemma showed no animosity towards her, just a casual friendliness and it occurred to her that Gemma did not see in her any threat of becoming a stepmother. It made her wonder if Matt had said anything to Gemma on that vexed question.

Then at the end of July, events moved quickly and a triumph was to be followed by a disaster.

Nicky was painting all hours of the day; she wandered around London, its parks, its pleasant squares, its docklands, looking for inspiration and in a strange way, far from her native Northumberland with its rugged fells, she found it and she did some good work. Matt was delighted.

He was pressing a friend who owned a small gallery near the Kensington High Street and a date was finally arranged for Nicky's exhibition. Nicky was in a torment of expectation and anxiety and when the paintings were finally carried from her studio to the Mulliner Gallery, her mood changed to one of doubt and depression. Even Matt couldn't shake her out of it; she felt sure the exhibition was doomed to failure.

Her parents were coming down for the opening and she put them up in Lacey Street; they seemed more than pleased to meet Matt again and made an extraordinary hit with Gemma. Their house was on the edge of Hexham and in farming country, it only needed an invitation to Gemma to spend a week up there with them to make Gemma wild with excitement. Matt looked on at all this with some amusement and teased Nicky about it.

"Gemma seems to have adopted your folks as grandparents," he said to her.

Nicky looked at him quizzically. "And what is that supposed to mean?"

He dropped a kiss on her forehead. "I'm wondering if it means I ought to ask you to marry me."

Nicky laughed. "Matt, I'm certainly not going to marry you so that Mum and Dad can become Gemma's grandparents. She's got perfectly good grandparents with your mother and father and you know it."

"I love to tease you, Nicky; seriously I'm very pleased that Gemma is going to have a week or two in Northumberland. I was going to find it difficult to leave London this summer." He looked at her. "Are you all ready for the big day?"

"I'm terrified."

He put an arm round her and hugged her. "I'll take care of you but no more holding hands for the press men."

"Oh, Matt, that was dreadful."

When the day of the opening of the exhibition came, Nicky was in a dream. She talked to people she did not know and wasn't sure if what she said made sense; she could see Gemma enjoying herself with her parents and Matt was everywhere. Archie Mulliner himself — he was a man of about sixty with very white hair — talked to the press and at the end of the day declared himself delighted. The notices that appeared in the papers during the next few days were favourable and Nicky heaved a sigh of relief; she felt she had done the right thing in coming to London.

Her parents went back to Hexham having made the arrangements for Gemma's visit in August, and all seemed right with the world.

Nicky's calm and sense of satisfaction were rudely shattered by the ringing of the phone in the middle of the night the following weekend; it was, in fact, early Sunday morning. She had no extension in her bedroom and ran down the stairs in a daze, thinking it was sure to be a wrong number.

"Nicky." A voice full of tension and anxiety.

"Matt, whatever is it? Is something wrong?"

"It's Gemma."

"Gemma? Whatever has happened, Matt?"

"She hasn't come home . . . I seem to have been waiting for hours . . . all I could think of doing was ringing you . . . "

"Matt, stop a minute and tell me exactly what has happened."

"She went to a party last night, someone's birthday. It was in the local sports hall, they've got a bar there."

"But Gemma's under age."

"I know, I know, she always has fruit juice, she's quite good about it; well, the party finished at twelve but she didn't turn up, I went round to the hall but it was deserted so I came back and I've just been waiting and waiting. What shall I do, Nicky?"

"Matt, just stay by the phone in case she rings up. I'll come over straight away."

"Oh, Nicky, thank you."

It took Nicky only ten minutes to get dressed and to drive over to Malton Square; Matt let her in and he looked dreadful. His hair was untidy, his eyes were dark. He took Nicky through into the kitchen where the first thing she did was to put the kettle on.

"We'll have some coffee," she said, "then you can tell me."

They took their coffee mugs through to the front room where the phone was and sat side by side on the settee.

"Tell me what you have done, Matt, and how Gemma was supposed to be coming home."

"Sarah Ketch's father was going to bring them but I've rung him and apparently Gemma and Sarah got separated and Sarah thought that Gemma must have gone home with someone else. There were a lot of cars outside the hall and Sarah wasn't worried."

"But Gemma didn't come?"

"No, I don't know whether to phone the police or not or to ring round the hospitals. I feel so helpless, and guilty, too."

"Oh, Matt, you can't feel guilty, you

had made a proper arrangement for her to come home and you've waited up for her. You could have gone to bed and not woken until morning and then found she hadn't turned up."

Matt was frowning. "Well, what do you think could have happened? Surely she wouldn't have tried to walk home alone and has come to grief?"

Nicky was thoughtful. "I think the most likely thing is that she's gone home with a friend and stayed the night; she's probably fast asleep in someone's house and will ring first thing in the morning."

"But it's not like her, Nicky, she's always been so careful to let me know where she is. She's been very good about it, I've never had any trouble before." He broke off and she could sense his distress. "It all comes with her having no mother, a girl needs a woman she can talk to."

"No, Matt, don't reproach yourself, you've been a wonderful father to her and she adores you. And it's

109

well known these days that young teenage girls don't take their mothers into their confidence, it's the exception rather than the rule." She held out a hand to him and he grasped it firmly and gladly. "We've got to be practical about it; what about the police?"

"I suppose I'd better ring them, I wish I didn't have to."

"No, you must, Matt, I'm not going to offer, there would have to be so many explanations."

He found the number of the local police station and Nicky could hear a short conversation. When he put the phone down, he turned to her. "They are sending someone round," he said grimly.

Within five minutes, a young constable and a WPC were in the room with them. They took careful details, were very considerate but not inclined to worry. It happened nearly every Saturday night, a girl went to a party and then stayed at a friend's house without thinking to ring home; often they were afraid of disturbing parents after they had gone to bed. But all checks would be made and they would report back as soon as possible.

They were back within half an hour and Nicky gave them tea. They had nothing to report, there had been no road accidents, one incident of youths fighting but no girls involved, and they advised Matt to try and get some sleep. They would come back at 8 a.m. but if there was any news either way in between, each must keep in touch.

Matt grinned ruefully when they had gone. "They were doing their best but how could they expect me to sleep? Do you want to go home again, Nicky, I can't keep you here?"

"No, of course I don't," she replied. "I'm staying with you. Why don't you put on a CD or a tape and we'll have some music, that might help us to relax."

But in spite of the music, Matt was on edge and seemed to want to talk, all about Gemma and Elaine and Laura.

Nicky listened drowsily and it was only the shrill ringing of the phone that made her realise that she had dropped off to sleep, her head on Matt's shoulder. She looked at the clock; it was seven o'clock in the morning. The dreadful night was over and she listened to what Matt was saying.

"Yes . . . Who? . . . You've got her there? Where the hell are you?"

Then a long silence and the sound of a male voice at the other end.

"Thank you very much, I'll come and fetch her straight away. 27 Dover Gardens. Thank you."

He turned to Nicky and held out his arms, she thought he had tears in his eyes.

"Where is she?" she asked.

"She's with a boy called Mark Rodwell, apparently she passed out on him and he didn't know what to do so he took her home with him. She's only just come to and told them who she is. He phoned straight away.

That's all I know. He sounded a decent lad." He was holding her close. "Will you come with me, Nicky?"

She looked up quickly. "Matt, I can't, it wouldn't be right."

"Please, Nicky, we don't know what's happened, she may need a female shoulder."

"OK then, if you really want me to."

Dover Gardens wasn't far away and a tall, fair-haired, young man opened the door to them.

"My parents are looking after — er, Gemma, but I thought I should explain first. I'm Mark Rodwell."

Inside the house, he spoke quietly and quickly.

"We were all at this party and although there was a bar, not many of us were drinking as we were most of us under age. But there were one or two gatecrashers, older than us and they'd obviously been somewhere drinking already. They made a fuss of the girls and . . . well the girls liked it. I suppose they thought it was grown up. I'd seen Gemma during the evening and I'd danced with her once, but she's not at our school and she didn't tell me her name. She was with another girl most of the time." He stopped and looked at them. "Sorry, it's taking a long time."

"It's OK, Mark, you're doing fine," said Matt quietly.

"When it came to 12 o'clock, there was a crush to leave, the gate-crashers were drunk and I swear they'd given some of the younger girls drink, too, as several of them were laughing hysterically. Well, I was about the last to leave, I've got a car of my own and I got outside and there was this girl on the ground; I thought she'd fallen so I bent down to help her up but she was a dead weight and I realised she was pissed . . . sorry, drunk or something. I couldn't wake her up however hard I tried. By this time, there was no one else around so I got her up and tried to get her to walk, she just made it to my car and collapsed into the passenger seat, all I could do was to bring her home here." He stopped again but no one made any comment. "My parents were still up and my father carried her in and asked what had happened. Oh, I should explain that my father's a doctor; he had a good look at her, didn't think she needed hospital or anything, so we put her to bed. Then, just before seven o'clock this morning, I heard her crying and Mum went into her. She remembered her name and everything, but couldn't remember passing out and she was terrified about what you would be thinking, Mr Hunter."

"And where is she now?" asked Matt.

"Mum and Dad are with her in the kitchen giving her some tea. They thought I ought to speak to you first. Shall I go and get her?" He looked at Matt very seriously. "You won't be cross with her, will you?"

"No, I won't be cross."

Gemma came into the room with

Mark's mother and father, her face was white; her eyes were red, her hair was all over the place and she looked dreadful.

She flung herself at Matt and he held her tight. "Oh, Dad, I'm sorry, I'm so sorry, I don't know what happened. And these people have been so kind to me and I don't even know who they are."

Dr Rodwell and his wife introduced themselves and Nicky was introduced as a friend of the family.

The doctor was kindly and matter-of-fact. "I think I guessed what had happened to Gemma as soon as I saw her, and what she has just told us bears it out. She doesn't want you to think she was drinking but I think one of the gate-crashers that Mark will have told you about laced her orange with vodka. Gemma will tell you the rest."

Gemma sat between Matt and Nicky and held on to both of their hands. "It's true what . . . Dr Rodwell says, I was with Sarah and these older boys came and sat with us, they were all right and I got up and danced. Then I finished my drink of orange and I started to feel queer; so one of the boys brought me another orange and I thought I should feel better for a drink but I felt worse. I had an awful head and the room seemed to be going round; then one of the boys said I'd better take some aspirin for my head and he fetched me two tablets and I took them. Then they wanted me to go home with them but I wouldn't and I was arguing with them and everyone was leaving. I lost sight of Sarah, she just didn't seem to be anywhere. We were all in a crush outside the hall and they were locking the doors, that's the last thing I remembered, the doors being locked. But Mark says he found me lying on the ground so I must have passed out. Then I don't remember anything else until just now and I woke up and I wasn't at home. I started to cry and Mrs Rodwell came in."

She looked around her. "You are all

looking at me, did I do something dreadful?"

Dr Rodwell leaned forward and talked to both Gemma and Matt. "I think that what happened was that they gave her the vodka and then a drug of some kind. I'm afraid it's a favourite trick at parties, it usually gets the girl on a high and she'll do anything. But it had a bad effect on Gemma and she passed out; that scared them and they ran off. Fortunately Mark was around when it happened and had the sense to bring her here."

Matt got up and shook his hand and then turned and shook hands with Mark. "I just don't know how to thank you. About the drugs, Dr Rodwell, will she come to any harm? Do you think I should take her to the hospital?"

Dr Rodwell shook his head. "One or two tablets like that won't harm her, it was probably mixing it with the drink that caused her to pass out." He grinned suddenly. "One thing is certain, I don't think that Gemma will

118

be tempted to take drugs or won't even drink in a hurry."

"No, I won't," said Gemma. "I'm feeling better since I had the tea, but it's funny, I feel like going to sleep again."

"Let's get you home, young lady, we've got to phone the police to let them know you are safe."

She looked at him in horror. "You never got the police in, Dad."

"Well, you could have had an accident," he replied. "We weren't to know."

They all walked to the front door and Matt thanked the Rodwells once again.

Gemma sat in the back of the car with Nicky and held her hand. "I'm glad you are here, Nicky," she whispered.

She slept for the rest of that day, had a bath, changed and had a good meal and said she felt a lot better. During the evening, Mark Rodwell appeared with a bunch of flowers and Nicky saw a pink flush of pleasure in Gemma's cheeks. It was to be the start of a good friendship between the pair of them until they went their separate ways to university.

Nicky had stayed at the house for most of the day at Matt's request, going home in the afternoon to see Millie and give her some food. She and Matt hadn't said a lot all day as they dozed on and off after their sleepless night. The young WPC came round later in the day and took a statement from Gemma, it had not been the first time that members of a gang had gate-crashed youngsters' parties and tried to push drugs.

When Gemma had finally gone to bed, Nicky said she must go, but Matt persuaded her to stay another half an hour and have a walk in the garden with him. They strolled the length of the lawn in the cool evening air and hand-in-hand.

"What a day, what a night and day," said Matt. "I never want to go through anything like that again. And she's only fifteen, I've got three more years to go before she goes off to university and I know that even then I shall still have the responsibility." He stopped walking and took Nicky's other hand in his. "Three years of growing up then she'll leave and I'll be on my own, I don't know which is worse. Nicky, I've got to ask you, would you come and share those years with me and help me look after Gemma?"

6

THERE was a silence around them in the garden, it was late in the evening, the only bird was a solitary thrush and it was almost dark. But there was no echoing silence in Nicky's mind after Matt's startling words. She was sure that Matt did not love her but he was asking her to share his life and also to share the bringing up of Gemma. Had she heard the question aright?

"Matt, whatever are you saying? You mean you want me to come here and look after Gemma for you?"

He shook his head and frowned; his hands still held on to hers and the clasp was tight. "I know it's mainly for Gemma's sake but I would like you for a companion, a partner I think the *in* word is. I can't pretend to love you, Nicky, but I am fond of you and you are lovely and very attractive and talented."

It was Nicky's turn to frown and she found rather to her shame that her voice was waspish. "So you want me to give up my own home, come and live with you for three years while Gemma is still at school, and after that time she'll be off and you'll be free."

She gave him a hard look. "Free to go off to Scotland and marry your Laura, I suppose."

"Nicky, that's ungenerous of you," he replied. "I mentioned three years because it's the time that Gemma will need a woman's influence. I can't get any further than that and Laura knows it, too, she understands."

"But what I can't understand is why you should think that Gemma will accept me in the house any more readily than she did Laura. You know what happened, you told me about it."

"Yes, I know, but Gemma is older and more reasonable now and I really believe she is coming to like you very much."

Nicky walked a few steps away from him remembering the first conversation she had had with Gemma. "But, Matt, she told me very definitely that she didn't need a mother, she'd got you and that was enough."

"I was hoping she might have changed her mind since getting to know you, Nicky." He came up behind her and took her arm. "Please think about it, will you? I won't rush you into deciding, just promise me that you'll think about it."

She was conscious of his touch and knew that it would be impossible to live with him without betraying her feelings. If he had said he had loved her and wanted to marry her then she would have thought differently, but she wasn't prepared to give up her home and her new-found independence for a relationship which wasn't based on love.

Nicky looked up at him then and

she thought the expression in his eyes was sad and lacked hope but it did not alter her decision and she found he was speaking again before she had a chance to reply.

"You are going to refuse, Nicky, I can see it in your face. I won't say anything more about it but we'll wait and see what happens when Gemma is with your parents. It's only another week now and you'll be taking her up to Hexham."

Nicky had offered to take Gemma and to stay on for a few days holiday and she guessed that Matt was thinking that not only might she get to know Gemma a little better but that she might miss him, too.

It was almost dark and she gave a little shiver in the cool night air. Matt put his arms around her and suddenly feeling very tired, she laid her head against him. "I'm a brute," he said and she felt him gently stroking her hair. "You've been here half the night and all day; your little cat will be wondering if she's been abandoned and here am I worrying you with my problems." He tilted her head towards him and touched her softly on the lips in a kiss that for once had no demanding passion.

"Matt, I'm sorry I can't say yes," she said quietly. "You will probably think I'm very old-fashioned when I say I suppose I am waiting for love and marriage but that's the way I feel."

"But Nicky . . . "

"No!" she interrupted quickly. "It's my last word and I think we are both tired and I must be getting home."

He saw her off and there was affection between them in their farewell kiss; the experience of the night and day had brought them closer together but as Nicky drove home, she knew that it was not enough.

Gemma's visit to Hexham was a resounding success. Nicky drove her north and found that Gemma was quiet during the long journey. They played tapes, both classical and pop, as Nicky had told Gemma to bring some of her favourite ones for the journey.

Her parents were both well and pleased to receive Gemma into their home; Mr Greenhowe had one more year to go before retiring as head of the local high school. He was a scientist and a naturalist and Gemma sensed his interest straight away and soon lost her shyness. Nicky's mother was a community nurse at a doctors' practice in Hexham, working just three days a week and hoping to retire at the same time as her husband.

Nicky stayed a few days and did some painting but she soon knew that she need not worry about leaving Gemma for two weeks, the girl blossomed under her eyes and it gave her a strangely reassuring feeling that Gemma was getting on so well with her parents.

Back in London, she found Matt in an odd mood; she discovered that he had been up to Edinburgh on gallery business and guessed that he had spent the time with Laura, though he made no mention of her. She also guessed that he was missing Gemma and did not like being in the big house on his own. He spent a lot of time in Lacey Street in the evenings when she was pleased to have him for a meal; he was friendly but somewhat distant and Nicky thought she could detect a certain resentment that she had not agreed to go and live with him. By the end of the fortnight, she discovered she was wrong but it took Gemma's return to bring out the truth.

Gemma had enjoyed a wonderful two weeks and Nicky thought it was obvious that her parents had spoiled the girl as though Gemma was their own grand-daughter. On the way back, Gemma hardly stopped talking and Nicky was amused at the difference in her.

As soon as they were out of Hexham, her young companion dropped the bombshell.

"Nicky," Gemma was speaking with excitement and enthusiasm, "your parents are great, they said I could call them Gran and Grandad after the first day. Wasn't that nice? Mr and Mrs Greenhowe sounded so formal. But do you know, I felt as though I could really have been their grand-daughter, they were so kind. Nicky . . . ?" She stopped suddenly and there was a query in the way she had said Nicky's name.

"Yes, Gemma?"

"Well, I was thinking if you married Dad, they really would be my grand-parents, wouldn't they? For keeps."

Nicky almost stopped the car at the side of the road; they were still on the A68 to Darlington and they had a long way to go before they reached the A1.

Did Gemma know what she was saying, Nicky thought, but the young girl had spoken in earnest and was waiting for a reply.

"But, Gemma," Nicky fought for the right words. "Do you realise what you are saying? It might be nice having Mum and Dad for grand-parents but you have always said that you didn't want a mother."

There was a silence between them. Then Gemma spoke slowly. "I know, I don't want a mother really but it might not be so bad if it was you, Nicky. You aren't like Laura and those awful boys."

Things were getting difficult, Nicky wished she knew what had happened between Matt and Laura on his visit to Edinburgh.

"Gemma, you've got to consider that your father might love Laura and want to marry her one day."

The silence was even longer this time and when Gemma spoke, it was with a certain air of defiance.

"Dad tried it before and it didn't work, I don't think he would marry anyone if it upset me," she said.

"Do you mean it wouldn't upset you if your father married me and not Laura?"

"Well, not as much. Does Dad love you, Nicky?"

"No, he certainly doesn't," replied Nicky quickly.

"Oh, I thought perhaps he did, he likes you a lot though."

How much can a girl understand, wondered Nicky, she's not sixteen yet but they seem to grow up so quickly these days.

"Liking is not the same as loving, Gemma, you will find that out when you are older."

Gemma gave a little laugh. "I've found it out already with Mark. I really like him and it's great to have him for a friend but I'm not in love with him."

Nicky tried to hide a little smile. "I think that is how your father feels about me, Gemma."

"He hasn't asked you to marry him, Nicky?"

"No, he hasn't asked me to marry him." Gemma seems to have no inhibitions about what questions she asks, Nicky mused.

"If he did, would you say yes?"

"No, I don't think I would, Gemma."

"Oh well, that settles it." Gemma's tone was final and not in the least bit concerned. "As long as he doesn't marry the dreadful Laura and I can keep Gran and Grandad Greenhowe, everything's all right." And abruptly, she changed the subject. "Nicky, you'll never guess what Grandad did, he's a hero."

Nicky gave an inward chuckle to hear her serious father being described as a hero. "What was that?" she asked.

"He arranged it with a friend of his who is a vet so that I could go into the surgery for a few days. Kind of work experience. It was fantastic, Mr Leadley, the vet, even let me watch an operation and I had to wear a mask. And I looked after the animals in the waiting-room, one dog was run over and had a broken leg."

Nicky knew that Gemma would go on talking all day about her experiences and only half-listened. Her mind was still on the previous conversation and

Gemma's seeming change of heart. But it didn't alter her own feelings on the subject; she knew she loved Matt, she had come to care for him very deeply but she would never marry him if he didn't love her, not even for Gemma's sake.

" . . . and on the last day, Mr Leadley talked to me about being a vet and all about the training. He said I had the right attitude and that I ought to work hard at my GCSE's and my A levels. So I'm going to."

The rest of the journey passed uneventfully and when they arrived in Malton Square, Nicky was touched to see the reunion between father and daughter. She was invited to lunch the next day and went home wondering if Gemma would repeat any of the pertinent questions she had asked Nicky.

After lunch, Gemma went off to see her friend, Sarah, and Matt suggested that they took the car down to Marlowe and had a walk along the river there.

He knew a little village pub by the waterside and later on they could have a quiet drink and perhaps a snack.

Nicky was pleased to agree and it didn't take them long to get out of London even though everyone seemed to be heading in the same direction on a fine afternoon in late August. When they arrived at Weston-on-Thames, Nicky could hardly believe that it was possible to find such an unspoilt rural place so close to London. There was no more than a small church and a cluster of houses and cottages with gardens running down to the river and the pub itself was surrounded by trees at the water's edge.

It was green and cool under the trees and the water lapped gently past adding to the peacefulness of the scene. Nicky slipped her hand into Matt's and they walked for a long way without saying anything. When they reached a fallen tree just off the path, Matt looked at her.

"Shall we sit down for a little while, Nicky? We've got plenty of time. You've been very quiet, what have you been thinking of?"

Nicky spread her jacket on the thick bark of the tree and sat close to Matt; she felt as peaceful as the scene around her and somehow didn't want to break the spell with words.

"I suppose I've been thinking about Gemma more than anything," she said to him. "She enjoyed her visit, didn't she, Matt? Did she tell you all about it?"

He grinned. "She hasn't stopped talking since she got back and all the grisly details of her days with the vet, too! She thinks the sun shines out of your father's eyes. But apart from her fantastic, as she put it, visit to the vet's, she also had a lot of things to advise me about."

Nicky's heart sank, it sounded as though Gemma had said as much to Matt as she had to her in the car coming home.

"She said a lot to me, too," she admitted.

"She seems to want your parents as real grandparents, that came over very strongly. They were very kind to her, weren't they?"

"Yes, I think they were inclined to spoil her, they've never had any grandchildren. My brother is married but they have no children as yet, I expect they will one day."

Matt suddenly slipped his arm around her shoulders and held her tight. "I think we've got to talk, Nicky, that's one of the reasons I brought you here, away from the house, sometimes it's easier to think in the open air, I don't know why."

She glanced up at him. She could guess what was coming and had the feeling that they were in for a difficult scene.

"You are very quiet," he murmured, his lips against her hair.

"I was wondering if some things are better left unsaid."

He shook his head. "No, Nicky. I've done a lot of thinking these last two weeks on my own. I didn't like being on my own, you know."

"You've got used to having Gemma around, it was bound to feel strange," she said.

"Yes, I know that and I suppose I should get used to it but I don't want to. I am only thirty-three and it's not my intention to spend the rest of my life on my own."

Nicky risked the next question. "And what about Laura, Matt, you went up to see her?"

He looked at her. "I suppose it got you curious, well if you must know. It was a disaster and I was knocked for six. You might have noticed that I was quiet when I got back."

"Yes, I did."

"I'd better come clean; I've always thought I would marry Laura one day when the children are grown up, hers as well as Gemma, I mean. I had a strong affection for her from the start

137

and we have a lot in common."

Nicky felt as though he had hit her, she had known he was attached to Laura but had no idea of the strength of his feelings. And why on earth had he asked her, Nicky, to go and live with him if that was what his plans were?

"But, Matt, you asked me . . . "

He wouldn't let her finish. "I know what you are going to say, why did I ask you to come and help me with Gemma if I had the intention of marrying Laura one day? I'm not as rotten as you must be thinking. Nicky, I dread these next few years with Gemma growing up and I really thought she liked you and you liked her. What would have happened at the end, I've no idea, I wasn't thinking that far ahead. But I knew that Laura was always there, it was something in the future, not now. But you refused me, didn't you?"

"Yes, I refused, Matt."

"Well, I thought I'd go and see Laura. She needs help with the boys and I thought perhaps we could have another go. It's five years since we tried before . . . " his voice trailed off.

"And?" Nicky prompted him when he stopped speaking.

"What I found in Edinburgh just about put the hat on any hopes I might have had about Laura. I'd always thought she'd returned my feelings but things can change in five years."

Nicky was curious. "What happened?"

"I found that Stuart and Ian now have a social worker after their latest exploits; he is Laura's age, unmarried, no children or ties, a very nice man who gets on fine with the boys. He and Laura have fallen in love and are going to be married next month. Laura asked me to go to the wedding."

Nicky could understand the bitter note in Matt's voice and she slipped her hand through his arm and reached up and kissed his cheek.

"I'm sorry, Matt."

"I was sorry, too. Sorry for myself and you noticed it." He turned her to face him. "Nicky, I've thought and thought and now Gemma coming home and saying she'd like you for a mother and your parents for grand-parents, yes she did say that to me, has made me decide."

Nicky felt herself go tense. "And what have you decided, Matt?"

"Nicky, I can't pretend I love you but I am very fond of you and . . . Nicky, would you marry me?"

She sat still and tried to stay calm for her main feeling was one of anger and that surprised her. For this was a selfish Matt, wanting her to look after Gemma, wanting her to ease his loneliness, it didn't seem to matter what her feelings were. For a moment, she despised him and then suddenly with a great rush of emotion, she knew she loved him for his weakness, for his care of his daughter and most of all because he was Matt.

"You're not saying anything, Nicky."

She stood up then and looked down at him and she saw the surprise in his face before she had even spoken.

"Matt, let's get this straight. You are asking me to marry you though you don't love me."

"Yes, Nicky, but I am . . . "

"You are asking me to marry you because in a few years time you don't like the thought of being on your own." She didn't wait for a reply this time. "You are asking me to marry you so that Gemma will have a mother to advise her and take care of her. You've worked it all out very nicely, haven't you?"

Matt stood and faced her, he was angry, too. "Nicky, all that is true and it's true because I've been straight and honest with you. I've not pretended. I could have made love to you, I could have persuaded you that I loved you, but I didn't because I thought you liked honesty and frankness."

"So I do, but I also want to marry for love. When I marry, if I marry, it will be to someone I love and who loves me. I'm not prepared to marry anyone for convenience, so my answer is no, Matt, I'm sorry but I cannot marry you."

He was staring at her; her blue eyes were flaring with anger and emotion, her mouth set in a determined line as though she did not want to give away her true feelings.

"Nicky . . . " he said. "Nicky, you still love me."

Furious with herself for not keeping calm, she turned away from him and started to walk back down the riverside path. But he caught her up in seconds; his arms gripping her shoulders tightly, he turned her to face him. Then he was rough as he pulled her into his arms and sought her lips with his; the kiss was rough, too, seeking an answer from her and as she felt his close warmth, reluctantly she relaxed against him and returned his kiss. She was the first to pull away, and she felt as though at that moment she hated him for his power over her.

"Nicky, you do love me."

She found her voice at last. "Matthew

Hunter, I despise you, don't ever let me hear you mention marriage again. In fact, I don't think I ever want to see you again. Don't say another word. Just take me home."

She set off down the path almost running in her haste and distress. They got in the car and all the way back to London there was a stony silence, neither of them said a word. She scrambled out of the car at Lacey Street and ran into the house without even saying goodbye. When she got indoors, she burst into tears. They were tears of anger and love, of disappointment and of heartbreak; if only Matt had loved her it would have been a different story, she would have been pleased to have taken Gemma under her wing and to have made a new home with Matt.

But it was all over, finished; she would not see him again and she felt like running away. I feel like going right away, she said out loud, away from Matt, away from Gemma. Going somewhere to paint, to give me new ideas, perhaps I need it.

She made herself some tea and picked up the Sunday paper to look at the holiday page; if she could let her London house for a couple of months, why not try and get a holiday cottage somewhere? Her eyes ran down the column, Lake District, Northumberland — she gave a weak smile — several in Cornwall. And there her eye stopped, Cornwall would be just the thing, she had never been there and she had never painted seascapes; it would be a challenge. Not St Ives, she decided, there are too many artists there. One of the smaller places and the word Porthcowan caught her eye. Small fishing village, cottage to let, September and October, and it gave a phone number.

Nicky didn't hesitate and in ten minutes it was all fixed up. She would take the cottage in Porthcowan from September 1st to October 31st. She put the phone down and gave a shout;

I've done it. I must be mad but I'll be right away from Matthew Hunter and I'll learn to forget him again. I've got a week to let this place and get packed up.

In the end, she put the house in the hands of an agency and it was let by the end of the week. She agreed to let it go on the Saturday and to stay in a hotel in Cornwall for a couple of nights until she could move into the cottage.

Then she had to decide whether to let Matt know that she was going away, there were the paintings and the gallery to think of, and what about Gemma? All the week she was undecided and at the last minute the problem was settled for her by a visit from Gemma herself. She arrived in the middle of one evening, troubled and unhappy.

"Hallo, Gemma, come along in, you look bothered."

Gemma looked at her. "I am bothered," she said. "Dad is in an awful temper, we haven't seen you all

145

the week and I wondered if you'd had a quarrel."

Nicky wondered how much she could say. "Yes, I'm afraid we did quarrel, Gemma, and I'm going away."

"Going away for good, Nicky? Oh, don't say that." Then she stopped as though she didn't know how to say the next words. "Did you quarrel over me?"

"No, Gemma, it was something very personal and I don't intend to tell you about it."

"I'm sorry, Nicky. Are you really leaving here?"

Nicky smiled for the first time when she heard the forlorn note in Gemma's voice. "No, I'm going on holiday for two months, I've taken a cottage in Cornwall and I'm travelling down there on Saturday."

"Are you taking Millie with you?"

Nicky laughed. "Yes, I am, I've bought a travelling basket and I hope she behaves."

"Oh, Nicky, I shall miss you terribly.

Will you give me your address so that I can write to you?"

Nicky hesitated. "Well, I'll give it to you as long as you promise not to tell your father where I am."

"No, I won't tell him. It will be between you and me and I hope everything will be all right when you come back."

"Yes, I hope so, too." Nicky took Gemma to the front door. "Now off you go and leave me to my packing. I'll see you in two months' time. You can tell Matt I'm going on holiday but don't tell him where I am."

"I won't, Nicky, goodbye." The girl reached up to kiss her then ran down the steps and was off home.

Nicky stared after her; it's a shame it couldn't have been otherwise but it can't be helped. I shall soon be hundreds of miles away and I shall forget the Hunter family and their problems.

7

IN spite of it being the end of August and still very much the peak holiday season, Nicky had a good journey to Cornwall. She had chosen to travel after the rush hour in the evening and it proved to be a wise choice even though it was dark when she reached Porthcowan. She was very tired and she carried her case into the small hotel without bothering to look around first; Millie was curled up asleep in her basket and Nicky put her by the side of the bed. She had a good night's sleep and was woken next morning by the noisy sound of clamouring seagulls. She looked out of her window and saw with delight that she had a view over the harbour and that the small fishing fleet had just arrived back accompanied by what seemed to be thousands of seagulls wheeling and screaming overhead above the boats. It was a sound that Nicky was going to get used to and would associate with Porthcowan for the rest of her life.

After a good breakfast, she set off to explore the fishing village; it was indeed tiny, no more than a cluster of houses and cottages around the harbour and some bigger houses built on the hillside overlooking the bay. There were steep cliffs on either side of the harbour and a sandy beach reaching out to a reef of rocks that Nicky was told by the hotel owner led into the next bay; but always be careful to go at low tide, he said, and not to stay too long as it was easy to be cut off. Levans Cove on the other side of the rocks was very pretty and secluded and worth a visit.

There was also a good cliff walk to Polskerrit if she liked walking which would give her lovely views of the whole stretch of coast. Nicky was delighted and felt pressures and troubles dropping away from her as she went in search of the cottage she had rented.

She hadn't far to look for she found it to be the end of a row of small cottages which lined the harbour at the farthest point of the village; she moved in two days later.

Her instructions from the owner had been that the key would be left with Mr Craze in the next door cottage and Nicky went to seek him out straight after breakfast on September 1st.

The man who came to the door in answer to her knock was very striking in both stature and looks. He was an extremely tall man, with broad shoulders and a shock of white hair; but the face was tanned and unlined and when he smiled he looked no more than fifty years of age.

"Mr Craze? I'm Nicola Greenhowe, I was told to come and ask for the key of Cliff End cottage."

He shook hands with her and gave a welcoming smile. "I'm pleased to meet you, Miss Greenhowe; I'm Robert Craze, Bob to my friends."

"And I'm Nicky," she said, responding to his warmth.

"I'll go and get the key, Nicky, and show you round the cottage. I've always looked after it for Mrs Tregorran and I hope you'll come and tell me if there is anything you need. Have you got a car? There is a parking space at the back in what used to be the garden."

Nicky was delighted with the accommodation; although the cottage was tiny, the main living room ran from front to back and there was a large kitchen in which she could have her meals. Upstairs, there was only the one big bedroom, the smaller room having been turned into a bathroom. She was particularly thrilled with the view from the front window, she looked right across the harbour to the sandy beach and the headland of Levans Cove; the sea was calm but the waves broke with white spray over the rocks at the far end of the bay. The colours were beautiful, the blue-green of the sea contrasting with the red sandstone of the cliffs; the bright colours of the fishing boats made a focal point to the scene.

She turned to Robert Craze. "It's really lovely, I hope to do some painting while I'm here."

"Amateur or professional?"

She looked at him and laughed. "Why do you say it like that?"

"I'm an amateur, I paint for the fun of it," he replied. "But occasionally we have a professional here and we love to see their work. There's a small gallery at the top of the hill if you want to try and sell your work."

"Mr Craze, do . . . "

"Bob," he interrupted.

"Bob, I shall have to confess. I am a professional, as you call it, and I've just had a show in a London gallery, but I wanted to get away to something quite different. I've always lived in the hills or in the city, I thought that the sea would give me a new challenge."

Nicky suddenly found him very easy to talk to, she was going to like her big neighbour, she decided.

"I shall look forward to seeing what you do but don't be afraid that I shall be for ever on your doorstep. We keep to ourselves but we're always willing to help when needed."

"Thank you very much, I'll go and get my car now. I've also brought my little cat with me. She's not much more than a kitten but I don't think she'll cause any problems. Then I must go and buy some food. I was pleased to see that there is a good general store."

"Yes, there's not much they don't sell and I like to give them the custom. A lot of visitors go into the supermarket in Penzance but I don't think that's fair on the Kempes who keep the store. They've got a butchery as well and I can recommend it."

He was at the front door which opened straight out of the living-room and Nicky said goodbye to him and watched him disappear into his own cottage. What a nice man, she thought.

He seems to be a resident, I wonder what he does, he looks too young to be retired.

Nicky didn't pick up a paintbrush for several days; she walked along the cliffs enjoying the fresh breeze and the lovely views along the coast in both directions; she sat on the harbour wall early in the morning, fascinated by the arrival of the fishing boats and all the activities that followed; she even lay on a towel on the sand and did nothing but soak in the sun, feel the salt breeze on her skin and listen to all the sounds she was coming to associate with Porthcowan.

She did think about Matt, it was difficult not to in her idle moments. She thought about Gemma too, and realised that she had got very fond of the girl. She regretted her quarrel with Matt but had no regrets about coming away; wondering if Matt was thinking of her, even if he missed her; she could not stop herself from loving him and she knew that if she had just one wish it would be that he could come to love her; Matt's love would be worth waiting for. She smiled ruefully to herself; I suppose in a way I've been waiting for Matt's love for fifteen years, she thought, but it seems hopeless. He is too hard hit by his experiences first with Elaine and now with Laura, to even want to love again. His only real concern is for Gemma.

By the end of the week, she decided she had done enough thinking and must get down to some work. But she was not drawn to painting the usual views of the beautiful coastline and seascapes and found herself gravitating to the harbour each morning, in the end getting up as soon as the squealing of the gulls wakened her and hurrying out to see the fishing boats come in.

And after four weeks, all her paintings were of the same industrious scene. Vital, colourful sketches and paintings of the boats and the fishermen in all their activities. She was rather reminded of the time when, as students, she and Matt had been sent to the shipyard. And so she forgot her pre-occupation with green leaves and trees and wondered if Matt would be disappointed. She had sold one or two small pictures at the art gallery on the hill and there was a demand for more but she kept her larger canvases for the London galleries.

In that time, she found she was getting to know Bob Craze quite well and everything about him, she liked but he still puzzled her. Perhaps he is just very wealthy, she would say to herself, but she rarely saw him during the day and even wondered if he went off to work somewhere. They would meet in the evenings, sometimes to take a walk along the cliffs, sometimes to have a quick drink at the Cod and Lobster, the small village pub.

It was not until one evening when he invited her for supper that she discovered his secret.

He had knocked on the door at

about five o'clock, she was just getting herself a cup of tea. She opened the door to find him smiling but refusing to come in.

"Nicky, I've got a couple of dressed crabs. Would you like to come and have a salad with me later on? I've put a bottle of wine in the fridge."

She smiled with pleasure for she had eaten her meals on her own for over a month. "Why, I'd love to, Bob, thank you very much. What time shall I come?"

"About seven o'clock, would that suit you?"

"Yes, fine, I'll see you later." She shut the door and couldn't but help feeling pleased. Perhaps I've missed the social contacts, she thought, it would be nice to have a night out.

Bob's cottage was almost a replica of her own but she gave a gasp when she walked into the living-room for every wall was lined with books.

"Bob," she said, looking round her. "So many books, I'd no idea you were such a bookish person. What do you read?"

He smiled down at her; her eyes were showing a lively curiosity. "They are mostly reference books and travel books and some I've been using for research."

She was intrigued. "Research? Do you mean you do some writing? Is that what you do all day when I don't see you?"

He laughed. "Yes, Nicky, I'm at my word processor most of the day, it's quite hard work being a writer."

"But it's fascinating, Bob. I've never met a writer before; artists, yes, loads of artists, but never a writer. Would I know your books?"

He led her to the end of the room. "I don't know Nicky, it depends whether you read thrillers or not."

"Well, yes, I do sometimes," she said. "Do you write thrillers?"

He nodded and she could see a glint of mischief in his eyes.

"You're hiding something from me,"

she laughed. "Are you a well-known writer, you've got to tell me?"

He pointed to several rows of books all with new dust jackets and in different languages.

"Those are mine," he said. "I write under the name of Philip Duke."

She stared up at him and he was still smiling. "You are Philip Duke? I don't believe it. Why, he's as famous as Dick Francis."

"I don't write racing stories though, Nicky."

She was looking along the shelves. "No, I know that, I've read some of them. Each one is set in a different country. Do you mean that is your research? You've never travelled to all those places?"

"Never been out of this little cottage, Nicola."

She burst out laughing. "Robert Craze, you are a cheat, I always thought Philip Duke must be a great traveller to write like that."

"I like to think I can get the

atmosphere of a place," he told her.

"Well, you certainly succeed, you have given me a surprise, and here I've been wondering what kind of mystery occupation you had. I even thought perhaps you went off to Penzance to a job each day."

"I don't speak of it to many people, in fact you are honoured to be asked in to supper." He took her arm and led her through to the kitchen. "I hope you don't mind eating here, I haven't got a dining-table in the other room."

Nicky couldn't remember enjoying a meal more, the food was very simple but good and she found it more than interesting to talk to Bob Craze now that she knew about his writing activities.

She insisted on washing up and as she put the plates and dishes away, her eye was caught by a small picture hanging in the corner of the kitchen by the old-fashioned dresser. It was a harbour scene and it was one of hers. She called out to Bob who was making the coffee. "You've bought one of my paintings from the gallery."

He came and stood by her, looking at it. "Yes, I couldn't resist having a painting by my famous artist neighbour. It's very good, Nicky. Have you been doing all harbour scenes?"

She nodded. "Yes, it seems to have got me, I like the activity and the cries of the gulls and the coolness and light of the early morning. It really does inspire me much more than the beautiful views along the coast."

"Yes, I can see that; are you keeping your best ones for London?" he asked her.

"Yes, I suppose so."

"And when do you go back? I shall be sorry to lose you."

She looked at him. "I can't believe I've been here over a month, I go back at the end of October. It's only about three weeks more."

She found that he was studying her closely and wondered what was coming next. They had quite happily avoided any conversation that bordered on the personal.

"And are you married, Nicky? Do you go back to a husband and a family?"

She shook her head violently and looked rather reproachful. "I've been trying to get away from emotional issues," she said and when he looked crestfallen, she did make a reply to his question. "No, I'm not married but I was getting close to someone and we quarrelled so I came away. I suppose I was running away really but I'm more than glad that I came here."

"I'm glad, too, Nicky." She didn't want to hear the words but they were said in a matter-of-fact way with no overtures of feeling.

"I'm not taking any notice of that remark," she replied in what she hoped was a light-hearted tone. "And now it's your turn! You are not married, Bob?"

"Not many people know that I was married when I was very young and it didn't work out and there was a divorce. I've never met anyone else since and I seem to have been quite content with my writing. The only person who gets entertained like this is my agent. I'm a very solitary person really, but a happy one."

She looked at him seriously. "I wish I could live a happy, solitary life, but I always seem to get entangled. I envy you, Bob."

"Do you love him, Nicky?"

What a strange conversation, Nicky thought, it seems so easy to talk to Bob and he is such a surprising person. "Yes, I've loved him for a very long time but it is hopeless. I don't want to talk about it or even to think about it. I've managed to put it all to the back of my mind all these weeks."

She found that he was putting out a hand and taking hers in his. "I'm sorry, Nicky, I shouldn't have probed but I just felt I wanted to know a little about you."

She found his touch comforting,

almost fatherly and she smiled up at him. "It's all right, Bob, it's been nice talking to you and it's been a lovely supper. You must come back to me next week."

"Yes, I'd like that and perhaps before you go back, you'd do me the honour of showing me your paintings. I'd like that, Nicky."

She got up to go. "Yes, I'd love to show them to you. I'd like to hear what you think about them. I'm pleased with what I've done but perhaps I'm prejudiced!"

It was to be the first of many evenings spent together but never again did they get on to personal topics and Nicky was glad. She had become very fond of Bob and wanted no romantic attachments to spoil their friendship.

Life continued very smoothly and happily for Nicky until she suddenly realised that she had only just over a week left in Cornwall. And so she had to think about her return to London; somehow she would have to patch up her quarrel with Matt for she was relying on him to take some of her paintings for the Orion Gallery. But she had no idea how she could resume a friendship with him and refused to spoil her remaining days in Porthcowan worrying about it.

Then half-way through the week before she had to start thinking of her return, affairs were taken out of her hands in a quite unexpected way. She had been putting the finishing touches to a picture and was cleaning her brushes and hands when she thought she heard a knock at the front door. It's not Bob's knock, she thought. Who on earth can it be at this time? And she hurried to the door, her cleaning rag in her hand.

When she opened the door she was to receive a shock.

A girl stood there, in shabby denims and a black jacket; her hair was blowing in the wind, she was carrying a sports bag and she looked anxiously at Nicky.

It was Gemma.

Nicky cried aloud. "Gemma, what on earth are you doing here and how did you get here?" She hesitated. "Is your father with you?"

"Nicky, I'm on my own. Can I come in and I'll explain?"

"Yes, of course, come in. You'd better come through into the kitchen. I'm cleaning my brushes. I can't believe it." Gemma was smiling now that she knew that Nicky was not cross at her arrival and Nicky wondered what on earth it was all about. "Gemma, you've not run away from home, have you?"

"Well, not exactly," was the unsatisfactory reply. "I'd had a cold you see and been off school and I was fed up at home and I miss you and I wanted to see you."

Nicky wiped her hands. "You'd better go and sit in the living-room. You'll find Millie asleep in the chair, she's been staying out all night and sleeping all day. I'll make us some tea. It sounds as though you've got a lot of explaining to do."

166

They were soon sitting side by side on the settee and Nicky looked at Gemma. Something's happened, she thought. She looks older.

"Gemma, I'd better start by asking you if Matt knows that you are here."

As Gemma hesitated, Nicky began to feel alarmed. "You'd better tell me from the beginning, Gemma. Everything, please."

"It's hard to know where to begin," the girl said. "I suppose it started as soon as you went away. I know you told Dad you were going on holiday but I was the only one who knew where you were and I didn't tell him, honest I didn't. He got very moody and bad-tempered and some evenings he didn't even speak to me, weekends were awful. I spent a lot of time with Sarah just to avoid him but he didn't even seem to notice." She paused and was thoughtful for a moment then she continued briskly. "Well, last night was worse than usual so I decided to ask him what was wrong and was it my fault. No, he said, it's nothing to do with me. So I asked him if he was missing you and he just glared at me and didn't say anything. So I put my arms around him and said he could tell me; he gave me a hug then and do you know what he said?"

Nicky shook her head but was silent.

"He said, 'I miss her like hell but there's nothing that you or I or anyone else can do about it. So stop worrying your little head and go on up to bed.' So I didn't say anything else, just kissed him and went up to my room and I did a lot of thinking."

"And what did you think?" Nicky asked her gently.

"Well, I worked it out that if he missed you that badly, maybe he wanted to marry you but wouldn't ask you because of me. You see, I knew you'd quarrelled but I didn't know why. So as I was off school in any case, I thought I would come down and tell you what was happening and it would get me out of Dad's way too.

Perhaps he needs to be on his own."

Nicky looked at her sharply. "Gemma, how did you get here? Doesn't Matt know where you are?"

"It's all right, Nicky, I'm not that hare-brained. I got the train to Penzance and then came to Porthcowan on the local bus. I was lucky, there's only one a day and I only had to wait an hour."

"And your father?"

"Oh, I left him a note. I told him I was going away to stay with you for a few days and would come back at the weekend in time for school on Monday. I told him not to worry about me."

"But, Gemma, he doesn't know where I am, you said you hadn't told him. Or did you leave the address in your note?"

Gemma shook her head. "No, Nicky, I didn't, you made me promise not to."

Nicky groaned. "Oh, Gemma."

"But I gave it to Sarah, you see, I thought someone ought to know where

169

I was. I went to see her before she went to school, she promised not to tell him, too."

Nicky didn't know whether to laugh or cry. The girl had tried so hard; Nicky found herself really glad to see her but it meant she would have to phone Matt to tell him where Gemma was. And she didn't relish the thought of that and decided to wait until they had had a meal.

Gemma was helping her in the kitchen when the phone rang. It was usually Bob at that time of the evening and she answered quite cheerily.

"Nicky." It wasn't Bob's voice.

"Matt."

"Is that scapegrace of a daughter of mine with you?" He sounded anxious but not bad-tempered.

"Yes, she is here. I was going to ring you when we'd eaten. However did you find the number?"

"I hadn't a clue where you were and searched right through Gemma's room. She'll be furious but it's her own fault.

I didn't find it so I phoned Sarah to see if she knew. She wasn't letting on but I could tell by her manner that she knew something, so I asked to speak to her mother; Mrs Ketch said she'd speak to Sarah and ring me back. She did just that five minutes ago, gave me your number and I rang straight away. Is she all right, Nicky? She didn't say very much in her note."

"Yes, she's fine. What do you want me to do?"

There was a momentary silence.

"Nicky, would you mind keeping her until Saturday? I can't really get away until then. I'll come down to fetch her and take her back on the Sunday, then I will see you, too." Another silence. "I've missed you, Nicky."

But Nicky took no notice of the remark. "Yes, Gemma's welcome to stay, we'll see you some time on Saturday, then."

"Thank you, Nicky. Goodbye."

Nicky turned to an enquiring Gemma. "Is he cross with me, how did he find

171

out where I was? I suppose it was Sarah."

"Yes, he had the sense to ring them and Mrs Ketch gave him the address and telephone number."

"And can I stay, Nicky? Please say yes."

Nicky smiled. "You can stay, young lady, but I've no spare bedroom, so you'll have to sleep on the settee, it pulls into a bed."

"Oh, that's fine, in fact it's great. But, Nicky, if you are busy painting, you can leave me to myself, you know. I won't interrupt."

"Well, we'll see about it, maybe a few days off wouldn't hurt me."

She found she was going to enjoy those few days. It was now late October and too cold for sitting about on the beach so she took Gemma on trips to visit the area, something she hadn't done on her own; they went over to Penzance and spent a day at Land's End, which Gemma loved. On their last day, the morning was fine and sunny and as the tide was right, they decided to walk round into Levans Cove, taking a picnic lunch. It was something Nicky had promised herself she would do before she left Porthcowan.

It was a beautiful little cove and once they were there they were tempted to go round the next headland into St Madoc's Bay, a lovely long stretch of sand which invited quick walking in the sunshine and the south-westerly breeze. At the far end of the bay, they sat on the rocks and ate their sandwiches; they were in a sheltered spot and reluctant to move away but Nicky was concerned about the tide.

"Gemma, we mustn't sit here too long, it's getting on in the afternoon and I think the tide is on the turn. We don't want to get cut off at Levans Cove."

They set off back across the sands and hadn't realised quite how far they had gone. When they got to the end of the bay the water was just lapping the rocks and they had to take their shoes off and roll up their trousers and make their way slowly and carefully round into Levans Cove. Once they were in the cove, they looked at each other in dismay for the water was well up the tiny beach and the rocks at the headland to Porthcowan had disappeared. They were completely cut off.

8

GEMMA'S voice was a wail of distress.

"Nicky, we are cut off, whatever are we going to do?"

Nicky felt dreadful, she also felt very foolish. They had asked Bob about the tide before they had set off that morning and she had known what to expect. But it had been sheer stupidity to go on to St Madoc's Bay; as it was they only just made it as far as Levans Cove in time. She did a quick calculation of the tides and then looked around her; and her heart sank. The cove was surrounded by steep cliffs, there was no sign of a path up and no possibility of climbing the sheer rock face.

She turned to Gemma. "I'm sorry, Gemma, I misjudged the tide when we went on to St Madoc's. All we can

175

do is sit it out, I'm afraid. Let's walk up to the cliffs, we will be sheltered there."

"What time will the tide turn, Nicky?" Gemma asked in a small voice.

"I reckon we'll be able to get around the headland at about midnight," she said trying to sound cheerful.

"And I'm hungry now," was all Gemma could say.

Nicky couldn't help laughing. "We've still got some coffee in the flask and there's a bar of chocolate, so it will have to be emergency rations. Get out your waterproof and put it on straight away, put the hood up, that will help to keep you warm."

They settled down as comfortably as they could with their backs to a rock and the sand scooped out to take the shape of their bodies. They chatted cheerfully at first but as darkness fell, they became silent and huddled up closer together.

It was Gemma who broke the silence.

"Nicky, I wish you hadn't quarrelled with Dad."

Nicky could hardly see the girl's face but turned towards her. "What made you think of that all of a sudden?" she asked.

She felt a hand reach out to her and she gave Gemma a reassuring clasp.

"Things seem better when you are there, Nicky. I know what I said about not sharing Dad with anyone but with you it's different, I wouldn't mind you for a mother, Nicky."

Nicky didn't say anything; Gemma was probably feeling in need of some protection and she was the nearest person to hand. The girl might feel differently once she was back in London.

But Gemma continued. "In any case, I've been thinking, I'm sixteen now and I think I can see things differently. Dad needs someone for a wife, doesn't he, it's not right he should be on his own? I would like him to marry you, Nicky."

Nicky listened to this frank statement

but was saved from replying by a loud shout from straight above them.

"Nicky, hallo, are you there?"

She jumped up quickly knowing it was Bob's voice.

"Bob," she called out. "We're here, we got cut off."

"I thought so. Stay where you are, Nicky, we're sending a boat round. In about twenty minutes, I should think, be prepared to wade out to it."

"Thanks, Bob."

They took their shoes off again and walked down to the edge of the water and it seemed no time at all before they could hear the chug of a small motorboat. One of the local Porthcowan men helped them in and Nicky had never been so thankful in all her life to be in a boat and speeding back to safety and dryland.

Bob was there waiting for them and as they got out of the boat, he held out his arms to Nicky and she was glad of the warm hug from the big man; he hugged Gemma, too, and took them back to his cottage where he had hot soup and some food all ready for them.

Nicky looked at him with gratitude in her eyes. "When did you realise we weren't back, Bob?" she asked him.

"I came in to ask you in for a drink this evening as you'll be busy all the weekend once Matt arrives. When there was no reply, I guessed what had happened. I was pretty sure where I'd find you so I asked George to have a boat ready, then took the car along the top of the cliffs at Levans Cove. You heard me call straight away so it wasn't difficult."

"We'd have been there till midnight if you hadn't come, Bob, I'll never be able to thank you."

He grinned, looking at her with an affectionate and meaningful expression. "I could think of a way you could thank me but I'm not going to ask you."

She met his eyes and knew with a sense of sadness that he had become very fond of her. She went up to him and reaching up, kissed him on the cheek. "Thank you, Bob, I'm sorry."

No more was said and there was a feeling of understanding between them.

Nicky and Gemma slept well that night after their misadventure and Nicky found that she awoke with some apprehension about Matt's arrival. She did not know what time to expect him but imagined he would make an early start and reach them by lunch time; she planned the meal and was glad to be occupied during the morning getting it ready.

By two o'clock there was no sign of Matt and Nicky was glad she had planned a cold meal and that nothing was spoiled.

She could tell that Gemma was anxious and tried to put the girl's mind at rest.

"The lunch will have to keep till this evening, Gemma; your father has probably left it until this afternoon to travel down."

Gemma frowned. "It's not like him, he usually likes to make an early start when the roads are quiet." She looked at Nicky with a worried expression on her face. "Why don't we ring up Malton Square to see if he's left?"

Nicky nodded and gave a forced smile. "Good thinking, Gemma, I'll do it straight away."

But the phone rang and rang with that somehow unmistakable sound of a phone ringing in an empty house.

She turned to Gemma. "He must be on his way somewhere, the roads are probably very busy with it being a Saturday, we'll just have to be patient, Gemma."

But it was an uneasy afternoon; Gemma stationed herself at the window and Nicky made countless cups of tea but by the time it got dark there was still no sign of Matt.

Gemma started to cry. "Something has happened to him, I know it has. He would never leave it as late as this and if he had been held up he would have phoned us."

Nicky put an arm around her. "You are thinking he has had an accident, Gemma, but I don't think it can be that. Even if he was injured, he would tell the hospital to get in touch with us."

But there was no comforting Gemma. "He might have been killed," she sobbed. "And no one would know that we are here."

"Don't look on the black side." Nicky tried to sound confident. "I'm sure there must be a good reason for the delay, he might even have got held up at the gallery."

"But he would have let us know, Nicky, I know he would."

"I'll phone the gallery, there may be still someone there. It's worth a try."

But the gallery was apologetic, no, Mr Hunter was not there. He had said he was going to Cornwall for the weekend and would go in on Monday.

Nicky and Gemma looked at each

other. Nicky felt sick with worry but she knew she must try and hide her feelings. Neither of them felt like eating but Nicky insisted that they should try and have something of the lunch they had prepared for Matt.

During the evening, Nicky felt that she must talk to someone and, leaving Gemma half-heartedly watching TV and trying not to cry, she went next door to see Bob. He knew that she had been expecting Matt and was surprised when he opened the door.

"Nicky," he said when she was inside the room. "What is it? You look upset, you've not quarrelled with Matt again, have you?"

She took one look at his concerned face and threw herself into his arms; he held her tight and she let herself cry for the first time.

"I wish I had quarrelled with him," she sobbed, "at least it would mean that he was here. He hasn't come, Bob, and we can't get in touch with him and he hasn't contacted us, we just don't know what has happened. Gemma's thinking the worst and, oh Bob, I just don't know what to think. What shall I do?"

"Hush, Nicky, don't cry like that, let us think. First of all, do you think your phone is working all right? Could he have been trying to get in touch with you and couldn't get through?"

She looked up at him and dried her eyes. "I never thought of that, I've been making outgoing calls. I'll run back to the cottage and you ring me up."

She flew back into Cliff End cottage but the phone was ringing by the time she opened the door and Gemma was rushing to answer it.

"It's Bob, Gemma, he's trying the phone to see if it's working all right. I'll answer." Nicky picked up the phone. "Hallo . . . yes, Bob, it's fine . . . yes, I'm on my way back." She turned to Gemma. "I won't be long."

Back in Bob's cottage, she found strong coffee and a glass of whisky waiting for her.

"Tell me what the arrangement was, Nicky," he said.

She told him and he thought carefully. "We have to face it," he said. "It rather looks as though he's had an accident and hasn't been able to get a message through to you. Have you tried the police?"

She shook her head. "I didn't see how they could help, if Matt's had an accident he could be in a hospital anywhere." She looked at him. "Gemma thinks he's dead."

"Poor Gemma, she's bound to think the worst at that age. Would you like me to try the police for you?"

"No, not tonight, Bob, but thank you. We'll try and get some sleep and then I'll ring the house again in the morning. If nothing has happened, I've got to think of what to do. But I'm glad you are here. You don't mind if I come in again in the morning?"

He put his arms around her and she laid her head against him and felt comforted. "You are to come in the

185

night if there is any news or you need me," he said. "Promise?"

"Yes, I will, thank you, Bob."

Nicky spent a restless night, half waiting for the phone to ring but Gemma seemed to sleep soundly.

While they were eating some breakfast, Bob arrived.

"No news?" he asked.

"No, nothing."

"Do you want me to get in touch with the police for you?"

Nicky looked at him but shook her head. "No, I don't think so. I've decided what to do, I've been thinking half the night. Gemma and I will set off straight away and get back to London. I worked out that if Matt's had an accident, he would have that address on him and that is where the police would be trying to contact us. Don't you think that's sensible, Bob?"

He agreed, "Yes, I think you are right, but you will go carefully won't you? And what about the cottage?"

"I'm due out on Tuesday but do you

think you could phone Mrs Tregorran and see if she'll let me have it for another couple of weeks? I don't suppose there's anyone else coming this time of year. Then I can leave all my stuff here and all being well, I'll come back next weekend."

He smiled. "So it's not goodbye?"

She reached up and gave him a kiss. "No, I'll see you next week. Thanks for everything. If by any chance, Matt does turn up today you'll tell him what we've done, won't you?"

"Yes, of course I will. Look, let me wash up and you two go and get your bags packed. The sooner you are off the better, it's only eight o'clock and on a Sunday morning the roads are pretty clear."

Bob proved to be right, the roads through Cornwall and Devon were quiet and soon they were on the M3, travelling quickly towards London. Gemma had hardly said a word, she sat in the back of the car nursing Millie and seemed locked in a world of her own.

At Malton Square, the house was shut up and Nicky was not surprised. Gemma had a key and it seemed strange to be letting themselves into an empty house. They looked carefully but there was no sign of any note or message and the only things out of place were the clothes in Matt's room as though he had left in a hurry.

Gemma was dark-eyed and looked at Nicky. "What do we do now?" she asked and her voice was flat and expressionless.

"I think I will phone the local police station."

Nicky made the call and five minutes later, a police car drew up outside the house. Gemma grasped Nicky's hand tightly as she opened the door to the uniformed constable and WPC.

"Constable Baxter and this is Constable Cunningham," the young man said. "Are you Mrs Hunter?"

Nicky shook her head. "No, I am a friend of Mr Hunter's. This is

188

his daughter, Gemma. My name is Greenhowe."

They all moved into the living-room and sat down.

"Mrs Greenhowe, we have been trying to contact Mr Hunter's family since yesterday afternoon. I'm afraid he has been in a road accident. Have you been away from home?"

Nervously and quickly, she explained the situation. Gemma was still clutching her hand tightly. "Is he all right? Do you know? He's not . . . he's not dead, is he?"

"No, Mrs Greenhowe, he's not been killed but he is seriously injured and in hospital in Basingstoke. The police from there got in touch with us, the accident was on the M3."

"Do you know how badly injured he is?" Nicky forced the words out.

"No, I'm afraid we don't." The constable seemed to hesitate. "Is there a Mrs Hunter? Do we need to get in touch with her?"

Nicky shook her head. "They separated

many years ago, she is in America. Can we go to him?"

"Yes, I would advise it. If you set off now, you can be there before dark, it's straight down the M3."

"Thank you very much."

Nicky saw them off in a dream then turned to hug Gemma to her. They both cried.

"Gemma, be brave, at least we know he is alive even if we don't know how badly injured he is. Get your case and anything you need, we may have to sleep in a hotel. I'll give Mrs Ketch a ring to explain. Have you got her number?"

Gemma gulped and gave Nicky the number. "But, Nicky, what about Millie, shall we take her around to Sarah?"

"Yes, good girl, I'll ask Mrs Ketch."

They left Millie at the Ketches and were soon speeding out of London again, Gemma sitting quietly at Nicky's side. Every so often she would say, "He's not dead, Nicky?" and once again Nicky had to try and be cheerful and reassuring which was the last thing she was feeling.

At the hospital in Basingstoke, they were told the name of the ward and were soon speaking to the sister at the nurses' station. She was a tall young woman, efficient and kindly at the same time.

"You are Mrs Hunter?" she asked Nicky.

Nicky shook her head. "No, I'm a friend of Mr Hunter, this is his daughter."

The sister looked straight at her. "Mr Hunter can only be allowed close relatives."

"But . . . " Nicky was at a loss for words. "Can you tell me how bad he is? I would rather be with Gemma when she sees him, she is only sixteen."

Gemma, who had just been described as only sixteen, suddenly took charge. "Nicola is going to marry my father so I think she should be allowed to see him.

In any case, I want her with me."

The sister smiled. "In that case, I will explain as we go along. Mr Hunter is in a side ward on his own, he was brought in yesterday morning and we've been trying to contact his family. I'm glad you are here, I think it's very important."

"But his injuries, are they very bad?"

"He has no internal injuries and no broken bones, but he is very badly concussed. I had better warn you that his coma is very deep, we have not been able to rouse him. On the other hand, he was given a brain scan and there is no evidence of any brain damage."

They had reached a door and she looked at the two of them. "We are hoping that if he hears the voices of someone familiar to him, he might respond." Then she spoke to Gemma. "Gemma, you must have courage for your father looks very bad and you might think he is dead, but I will let you feel his pulse and then you will know that he is alive."

Nicky had taken all this in with a feeling of sickness and dread and she took Gemma's hand and they followed the sister into the small room. A nurse who had been sitting at the side of the bed got up as they entered.

"No change, nurse?"

"No change, Sister."

"Mr Hunter's fiancée and daughter have arrived. I want them to sit with him so you may go now."

Nicky was glad of that short conversation for she had to come to terms with the fact that this had got to be a living Matt; his face was white and taut, his body rigid and she couldn't help the thought, he looked like a corpse. She glanced at Gemma but the young girl had thrown herself across the bed and was crying out, "Daddy, Daddy." She was half sobbing. "Dad, wake up, it's Gemma. And Nicky's here too."

There was no response from him and Gemma straightened up and faced the sister. "You were lying. He's dead. He looks dead."

The sister kindly put an arm round Gemma and got the girl to feel his pulse, then she put her hand on his chest which moved slightly as he breathed.

"Gemma," the sister said, "you must talk to him, about anything, just keep talking and saying his name. And you, Miss Greenhowe, tell him you love him, I assume you do if you are going to marry him. Anything to stir his sub-conscious. I will leave you now and there is the bell for you to ring if you notice any change, it doesn't matter how slight it is."

Nicky afterwards remembered those long hours in a daze. She spoke Matt's name, Gemma chattered endlessly, they had cups of tea and food brought to them then, as it got later, they were given a room near the ward in which they could sleep. They must sleep, they were told, for in the daytime they would be needed at his bedside.

For two days there was no change, and Nicky and Gemma took it in turns to sit at Matt's side in between going for a walk or having a cup of coffee in the refreshment room.

By Tuesday, Nicky was feeling tired and grim; Gemma was with Matt and Nicky was drinking coffee in the cafe oblivious to the people around her. She had heard of people being in a coma for years, what hope was there, though the doctors seemed to think he would be roused by some familiar touch or sound.

Suddenly she was seized in a hug by an excited Gemma.

"Nicky, come quickly, Dad said 'Nicky'. I know he did, I rang the bell and sister came and she told me to come and fetch you."

An hour later, they were both sitting by his side when they saw Matt open his eyes and say "Gemma."

She threw her arms around him. "I am here, Dad. It's Gemma. Please get better, oh please get better."

They watched him turn his head and he seemed to see them. "Gemma," he said. "Nicky."

They were both crying and the doctor came in and took over. By the end of the day, it seemed as though a miracle had occurred as they saw Matt propped up in bed taking a sip of tea and putting out his hand to each of them.

Another day and he was taking his first steps and the doctor was saying he should make a full and rapid recovery.

The first time he was on his own with Nicky, he held her hand. "It's funny not being able to remember," he said. "I do remember I was driving to see you and it was something to do with Gemma. And something was wrong, what was wrong, Nicky?"

"We quarrelled, Matt, perhaps I shouldn't remind you and I went away to Cornwall to paint. Gemma came to see me on her own and you were coming to fetch her back."

He looked at her. He was sitting in a chair by the bed and was beginning to look well again. "Why did we quarrel, Nicky? Sister refers to you as my fiancée, but that isn't right, is it?"

"Oh, Matt, you aren't well enough to talk about it."

"Tell me."

"You asked me to marry you and I wouldn't because you didn't love me; Gemma told sister I was going to marry you so that they would let me in to see you, but no, it wasn't right. You were very cross when I refused you."

"Oh."

"We mustn't talk about it now, you've got to get better."

By the end of the week, he was better and able to leave the hospital. Nicky drove him back to Malton Square amidst great rejoicing. He was determined to return to the gallery on Monday though he had been told to rest for another week.

Nicky found the atmosphere strangely strained between Matt and herself; she knew she was tired and over-reacting but there had been no words or gestures of affection between them and she was wondering if Matt had changed his mind about wanting her to marry him. She knew, if it was possible, that she loved him more than ever.

She decided to have her last week in Cornwall and to go down and bring all her paintings back. She told Matt about it when they were quiet after dinner on the Saturday; she had stayed the last few nights at Malton Square.

"Matt, I am going down to Cornwall tomorrow. I've got one more week of my letting left and I want to finish off the pictures I was in the middle of."

"And to see Bob?" He asked her and spoke rather slowly.

"Bob?" She couldn't think who he meant for a moment.

"Yes, this Bob I've been hearing so much about from Gemma; the man next door, the man who came to your rescue when you got stranded in the cove. He seems to feature largely in your Cornish holiday, Nicky, what does he mean to you?"

She looked startled, he sounded almost jealous and it explained the lack of communication between them since they had returned from the hospital.

She did her best to explain. "But Bob was only my next door neighbour, he's very nice. He's a writer, he writes thrillers, he's Philip Duke."

"Is he indeed? He's obviously made an impression on you."

Whatever is happening, Nicky thought desperately, it's not like it used to be and for the whole evening after that, Matt was polite and distant but Nicky could not tell what he was thinking. She was glad when the evening came to an end and she was able to tell him that she would not see him in the morning as she was going to make a very early start for Cornwall.

9

THE next morning, Nicky had a trouble free drive down to Cornwall and when she got to Cliff End Cottage, she went straight in to see Bob. He stood there tall and solid and his expression invited confidence; as he closed the door behind her, she threw herself into his arms and burst into tears. He held her close and she could feel the tenderness in his embrace.

"Nicky."

She looked up and saw what she did not want to see in, his eyes. "Oh, Bob, it's been such a dreadful week. It's lovely to be here again."

"Thank you for keeping in touch, Nicky. How is Matt now?"

"He's a lot better," she replied. "He is talking of going into the gallery tomorrow. He's not supposed to but

I expect he will."

"And all is well between you?"

She raised her head at his question, then shook it wildly. "No, it's not well at all. I'm such a fool, I love him so much and he doesn't seem to care a damn. We had an awful evening last night, it was the first time we had been on our own and it should have been so nice to be together again after all that had happened."

"Hush, Nicky, come and sit down, I don't like you to cry like that, no man is worth it." He stroked her hair and she let her face rest against him until the storm of weeping was over. "Nicky, I've got to ask you, couldn't you care for me instead? I've got so fond of you and we get on so well together. Would you marry me, Nicky?"

She looked up at him and wished she could have said yes, it would have made a comfortable way out of her problems.

But she shook her head. "I'm sorry,

Bob, thank you for asking me but I can't say yes."

"Is it because I'm a lot older than you, Nicky?" he asked her then.

"No, no, I don't think of age and I'm very fond of you, but being fond of someone isn't enough. I love Matt and if I can't marry Matt, I shall never marry anyone. She buried her face against him and his arms came round her again."

"And what makes you think that Matt doesn't love you?" he said.

"He told me so; he had that awful experience with Gemma's mother, then he got attached to someone else and she's just announced that she's marrying another man. I think that was the last straw. He asked me to marry him for Gemma's sake but I knew he didn't love me so I said no and we quarrelled and I came away. Then he had the accident and things haven't been right since and he's got it into his head that you are important in my life; well you are but not in the sense that he means."

He hugged her. "I wish it was me that could make you happy, Nicky, but I understand. I shall just have to go on being the lone writer!"

"I expect all your fans will be pleased," she said with a smile.

"That's better," he laughed. "Now I'm going to suggest that we have a meal together and then let's have a day off tomorrow, take the car over to St Ives and have a look round the galleries. You'd like that, wouldn't you?"

She looked at him gratefully. "I would, very much; thank you, Bob."

At the same time the next day that Bob was driving Nicky home from St Ives after their day out, in Malton Square, Matt and Gemma were spending their first evening on their own together. Both of them were very quiet at first, Gemma conscious that she had displeased her father when she had run away to Cornwall and been the unwitting cause of his accident, and Matt aware of the responsibility of having a teenage daughter. It was when they were having their coffee after their meal that they both seemed more inclined to talk.

"So you enjoyed your few days with Nicky in Cornwall then, Gemma?"

She glanced up at him but his face gave nothing away. She decided she would speak her mind even if it made him cross.

"Yes, and when we were marooned in Levans Cove we had a long talk."

"What was that about?"

"I told Nicky I wouldn't mind having her for a mother and I was sorry she had quarrelled with you." The words came out in a rush.

"You said what?" Matt's question was sharp and Gemma thought she was going to regret speaking her mind.

"I like Nicky, Dad; I wouldn't mind if you married her. I realise now that I've been selfish, you need someone, don't you?"

"Oh, Gemma, I would never marry

anyone if I thought it would upset you." He looked at her keenly. "But maybe it's too late, what do you think about Nicky and this Bob Craze?"

"Bob?" said Gemma in some surprise. "Nicky likes him, he likes her, too, he hugged her when we got off the boat when he rescued us. But I don't think he wants to marry her, he's too old. I don't know really."

"I don't either." Matt sounded grim and no more was said on the subject.

* * *

During her last week at Porthcowan, Nicky found it difficult to work and thought of packing up early. Bob had gone up to London for a couple of days to see his publisher, taking the train from Penzance, and she found she was missing him. On the second day he was away, she decided to clean through the cottage and start to pack up her things. She was busy upstairs in the bedroom when she heard a car pull up outside; it was mid-morning and she was puzzled, knowing it could not be Bob as he was taking a taxi home from Penzance late that evening. When she heard the hard knock at the door, she ran down the stairs quickly and opened it. When she saw who it was standing there, she gave a gasp.

"Matt."

He was smiling, he was handsome, he was carefree, he was the old Matt of years ago.

He stepped into the room without saying a word and he slammed the door shut behind him. Then she was in his arms and his mouth was hard on hers; Nicky felt a magic, an uplifting of spirits as she felt sure she could sense his love in the embrace. She couldn't believe she was in his arms, neither could she stop herself pressing closer to him and returning his kiss with all the love that had been waiting in her heart for so long. That she did not understand why he was here so miraculously did not bother her;

Matt had come at last. Then she was listening to his words.

"Nicky, don't ask any questions, nothing matters except that I love you and you say you love me and that you are going to marry me and almost the most important thing, Gemma is pleased about it."

She stood back and looked at him and burst out laughing. "Matthew Hunter, whatever are you doing here, you should never have driven all that way; and what are you talking about? Do I have any say in the matter?"

He held her hands and looked at her earnestly. "We have a lot of talking to do and I came just as soon as I could this morning. I got up at five and have driven very carefully, fortunately the roads were quiet."

"But, Matt, what on earth has happened? Everything was wrong when we got back from the hospital and I was so miserable."

"But you didn't say that you would marry Bob when he asked you?"

"Bob? Whatever has he got to do with it and how could you possibly know that Bob had asked me to marry him?" Nicky was more puzzled than ever.

"He's got a lot to do with it," Matt replied. "But, come, make me some coffee, get your jacket on and we'll have a walk over the sands. If the tide is right, you can show me this famous cove where you and Gemma got stranded."

She made him coffee and toast which was all that he would have, then he helped her on with her thickest jacket for the November wind was chilly and they set off, hand-in-hand, past the harbour and on to the sandy beach.

"Are you going to tell me, Matt?" Nicky asked tentatively.

"When we get to those rocks we'll sit down and I'll put my arms around you to keep you warm, tell you all about it and never let you go again."

Nicky could only think he must be crazy and was no nearer to understanding what had happened. They found a sheltered corner in the rocks and sat close together, looking at the waves breaking on the shore and the white clouds racing eastwards across the pale blue sky.

Matt spoke at last. "Nicky, I owe you a lot of explanations, can you bear with me? I've behaved abominably and I'm sorry we quarrelled, all I seemed to be able to think of was getting a mother for Gemma. I'd lost Laura and I suppose it was natural to turn to you, but we quarrelled, didn't we?"

"I'm sorry, Matt, but I couldn't have married you for Gemma's sake when you were saying you didn't love me. But I was glad I came away, I've enjoyed it here and I've done some good paintings. I think you you'll like them."

"Never mind about paintings," he said. "We're talking about us. After you'd gone on holiday, I missed you terribly, I can't describe it. I knew then that I loved you, that I'd loved you all those years and I couldn't wait for you to come back. Then Gemma disappeared and when I found out where she was, I knew it was my opportunity. I came racing down to you and had that terrible accident. All I seem to remember about it was when I came round, I didn't know it was days later, I could think only of you." He gave her a long searching look.

She smiled. "My name was the first word you said, Gemma was so excited, she was sitting with you at the time."

"As I got better, it was difficult to speak to you privately and a hospital somehow isn't the right place for telling someone that you love them. Then it all seemed to go wrong, Gemma kept talking about this Bob you had met and I really began to think you were fed up with me and had fallen for him . . ."

"But, Matt, I didn't . . ."

"I know, I know now but I didn't know then. Two things I didn't know, how Gemma would react if I said I was going to marry you and neither did I know how attached you were to this Bob."

"Matt, I keep telling you and you won't listen to me . . . "

He kissed her. "I want to explain first and then you can have your say. The first problem of Gemma was overcome after you'd gone back to Cornwall, she suddenly announced that she would like you as a mother and she wanted me to marry you . . . "

"I know, she told me, too," Nicky interrupted.

"But she wasn't sure how you felt about Bob; and I didn't know either; for all I knew he might have been very keen to marry you."

"He did ask me," she said.

"And you turned him down?"

She nodded. "But how did you know?"

Matt grinned. "Yesterday afternoon, I was at the gallery and I had a visit from Robert Craze."

"Bob came to see you at the gallery?"

"Yes, he did, we went into my office.

And he told me in no uncertain terms that you wouldn't marry him because you loved me and if I loved you, for heaven's sake get down to Porthcowan and tell you so. Here I am, and I want to know what you are going to say to me."

His arms had been holding her close and she pushed slightly away to look at his face. She saw the love in his dark eyes and it filled her with a great excitement; she reached up to him and gently kissed him on the lips, a gesture all of her own, caring and loving.

"Matt, I don't know where to start. It was very kind of Bob to come and see you, he has been a really good friend while I've been here but nothing more than that. There was never anyone else but you, Matt. I've waited all these years; as soon as I saw you again at the gallery, I think I fell in love with you all over again."

"But you wouldn't marry me?" he asked her.

"Not when you didn't love me," she replied.

"And now you know I love you, is your answer still the same?"

Nicky couldn't help laughing and immediately she was caught in a long and passionate kiss. When she got her breath back, she put her fingers on his lips. "I do love you, Matt, and I will marry you," she whispered.

His arms were crushing her but she loved their strength and what that strength told her.

Then she remembered Gemma.

"Matt, someone is going to be pleased!"

"Gemma?"

"Yes, I don't think I shall be the wicked stepmother do you?"

He touched her lips gently and lingeringly. "No, Nicky," he said. "We both love you."

WITH SOMEBODY ELSE
Theresa Charles

Rosamond sets off for Cornwall with Hugo to meet his family, blissfully unaware of the shocks in store for her.

A SUMMER FOR STRANGERS
Claire Hamilton

Because she had lost her job, her flat and she had no money, Tabitha agreed to pose as Adam's future wife although she believed the scheme to be deceitful and cruel.

VILLA OF SINGING WATER
Angela Petron

The disquieting incidents that occurred at the Vatican and the Colosseum did not trouble Jan at first, but then they became increasingly unpleasant and alarming.

DOCTOR NAPIER'S NURSE
Pauline Ash

When cousins Midge and Derry are entered as probationer nurses on the same day but at different hospitals they agree to exchange identities.

A GIRL LIKE JULIE
Louise Ellis

Caroline absolutely adored Hugh Barrington, but then Julie Crane came into their lives. Julie was the kind of girl who attracts men without even trying.

COUNTRY DOCTOR
Paula Lindsay

When Evan Richmond bought a practice in a remote country village he did not realise that a casual encounter would lead to the loss of his heart.

ENCORE
Helga Moray

Craig and Janet realise that their true happiness lies with each other, but it is only under traumatic circumstances that they can be reunited.

NICOLETTE
Ivy Preston

When Grant Alston came back into her life, Nicolette was faced with a dilemma. Should she follow the path of duty or the path of love?

THE GOLDEN PUMA
Margaret Way

Catherine's time was spent looking after her father's Queensland farm. But what life was there without David, who wasn't interested in her?

HOSPITAL BY THE LAKE
Anne Durham

Nurse Marguerite Ingleby was always ready to become personally involved with her patients, to the despair of Brian Field, the Senior Surgical Registrar, who loved her.

VALLEY OF CONFLICT
David Farrell

Isolated in a hostel in the French Alps, Ann Russell sees her fiancé being seduced by a young girl. Then comes the avalanche that imperils their lives.

NURSE'S CHOICE
Peggy Gaddis

A proposal of marriage from the incredibly handsome and wealthy Reagan was enough to upset any girl — and Brooke Martin was no exception.